PRETTY

Jeffrey DeShell

SPUYTEN DUYVIL
New York City

ISBN 978-1-963908-02-2

Cover Photo:
Five Girls in a Room in Pigalle, Paris—
© Deborah Turbeville/MUUS Collection

Library of Congress Control Number: 2024937732

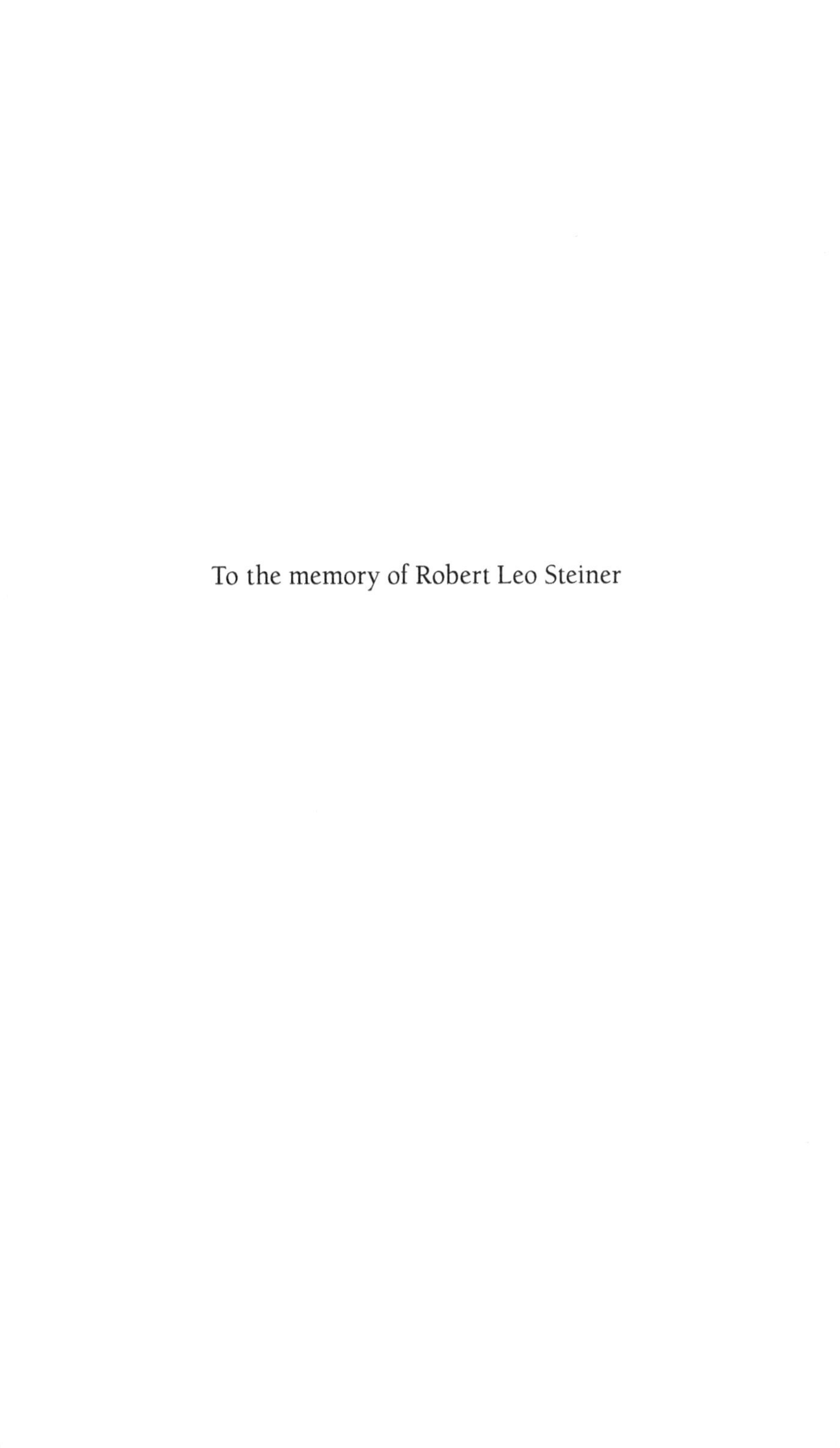
To the memory of Robert Leo Steiner

"Let us suppose Truth is a woman—what then?"
Friedrich Nietzsche

Millie (Millicent) **Isla Del'Aria** (born September 13th, 1971) is an American model and actress, who was active from the 1990's to 2004. She worked most prominently with the fashion designers Martin Margiela, Alexander McQueen, and Rei Kawakubo of Comme des Garcons. She was the face of the Hermès fragrance collection in 2002. Born to middle-class parents in the small town of Walsenburg, Colorado[1], Del'Aria rose to fame in Paris, where she was discovered by Martin Margiela at a bus stop.[2]

She became his 'fit model' and was soon walking the runway for Margiela, McQueen and Comme des Garcons in the 90s, and later Hermès in the early 2000s. She is best known as the featured model for the international Hermès fragrance campaign of 2002-03, in which she worked with the famous fashion photographers Steven Meisel, Juergen Teller and Ellen Von Unwerth.[3]

She retired from modeling in 2004. Del'Aria was known for her ability to portray both glamorous and down to earth types: Alexandra Shulmen, the editor of *British Vogue*, once said of Del'Aria, "Millie looks the Queen in one picture and a guttersnipe the next."[4]

---

1 *Millie Del'Aria*, from https://www.womenmanagement.fr/home.web, retrieved Feb 2nd, 2009.

2 Samson, Alexandre. "Martin Margiela: the Origin" in *Margiela: The Women's Collections*, Rizzoli 2018.

3 *Millie Del'Aria* models.com, retrieved October 19th, 2019.

4 Mason, Pamela. "Who's that girl? The New Face of Hermes." (Jan 2001) *British Vogue*, retrieved June 4th, 2017.

Millie (Millicent) Isla Del'Aria

> **Born:** September 13th 1971
>
> **Occupation:** Model, actress
>
> **Years active:** 1990-2004
>
> **Modeling Information**
>
> **Height:** 6' 0" (183 cm)
>
> **Hair color:** Brown
>
> **Eye color:** Green
>
> **Agency:** Women Management Paris
>
> **Contents**
>
> **Early Life**
>
> **Career**
>
> **Personal Life**
>
> **References**
>
> **Links**

EARLY LIFE

Del'Aria was born in Walsenburg, Colorado, to Inez Elizondo (schoolteacher) and Dominic Del'Aria (bartender). She has a brother, Carmine (b 1978), and a sister, Agnes (b 1981). She graduated from John Mall High School, where she got excellent grades and showed interest in foreign languages.[citation needed] She attended Adams State University in Alamosa, Colorado, for one year, where she majored in Spanish.[citation needed]

CAREER

After her initial year at college, while visiting her aunt in Paris, Del'Aria was spotted by the fashion designer Martin Margiela at a subway stop. He recruited her to model in his upcoming fashion show, which was held at a Parisian playground. Del'Aria soon became Margiela's muse and was his in-house model from 1990 to 1999.

She walked many of Margiela's runway shows, both for his eponymous house (Maison Martin Margiela) and the luxury label Hermès when Margiela was chief designer there. She also featured in the runway shows of Alexander McQueen and Rei Kawakubo of Comme des Garcons. Del'Aria starred in the multi-media advertising campaign for Hermès fragrances in 2002 and 2003, where she appeared in magazine print ads, billboards and television commercials. In September of 1995, she appeared on the cover of *Vogue Italia*, shot by Juergen Teller, and in January 2003 she graced the cover of *Vogue Paris*, working with the photographer Ellen Von Unwerth. She declined to renew her contract with Hermès in 2003 and retired from modelling in 2004.

PERSONAL LIFE

Del'Aria has always been fiercely protective of her privacy and has refused to give interviews or press conferences. She has no social media presence. She was arrested in London on drugs charges in 2000, but the charges were dropped.[5]

It was thought she may have checked herself into rehab in

---

5 "Models Arrested in Drugs Sweep," *The Guardian* (November 14th, 1999), retrieved April 1st, 2002.

2001, forcing her agency to issue the statement that "such baseless rumors and innuendo are as thoughtless as they are untrue."[6]

Del'Aria currently lives in Paris with her sister, where she continues to shun all media communication.

Rather humble beginnings, this lanky issue of a prairie schoolteacher and wild west bartender from a one-horse town in the middle of nowhere more or less. According to MapQuest, anyway. From Walsenburg to Paris, tumbleweeds to the Trianon, enchiladas to escargot: he guessed that could be an angle.

They were exactly the same age, the two of them, the model and her would-be Boswell, born the same day. Now, with fifty breathing down their necks, best years long dusted. At least for her anyway: fashion models usually aged out at twenty-five, so twice that likely offered few options. He, on the other hand, had a career: he would teach for another fifteen or so and had at least three book projects at various stages (one a novel!), depending on how much self-deception he entertained. Plus, he had kids, a family, a wife. And a dog. In other words, a life.

He had not looked at the photos yet, as he desired some context before he opened and ogled. He was skeptical of the whole fashion thing to begin with, and although he was sensitive to beauty in all its forms (so he thought), his

---

6 *Millie Del'Aria*, from https://www.womenmanagement.fr/home.web, retrieved July 17th, 2011.

knowledge of, interest in and patience for *couture* and its various industries was negligible. There was something truly obscene about the extravagance, about the money and attention paid to the spectacle of the ritualistic exhibition of skinny white women and their ostentatious frocking, a capitalistic atrocity that provoked feelings ranging from disgust to embarrassment to envy. Especially now that the world was beginning to burn. Neros, Neros everywhere.

Even in the best of times, he would be fantastically ill-suited to this assignment, this task of writing a biographical chapter of a forgotten and reluctant fashion model who was somewhat important to an avant-garde fashion designer of twenty to thirty years prior. He had only the vaguest idea of womenswear, and knew fashion post 60's but peripherally, seeing only an insistent devolution to gimmicky ugliness and a ubiquitous and self-deceiving machine dedicated to the "art" of fashioning surrealism into marketable commodities. What he could bring to the project— a notorious and indefatigable gimlet eye, a sympathy toward women skirting on devotion (which bordered on a banal and perhaps less virulent but still troublesome misogyny), and the capability, when moved, of composing insightful and sometimes lovely sentences—was likely irrelevant to the sugary con job expected. He didn't know the people, the language or the culture: he'd be a lazy and bored tourist in some flyover he'd only dimly heard of. Like Albania. He chuckled.

And these weren't the best of times. People were dying, according to the news, by the truckloads. He'd escaped the city upstate with his family, and they all remained healthy *al hamdu li'allah*. He and his wife could teach online, not happily, but they likely wouldn't take a huge financial hit. They weren't in the city, and they were Zooming classes, true, but other than that, the virus was largely virtual, confined to their collective screens beyond the walls of their Hudson Victorian. He remembered the Poe story and his Prince Prospero. He also remembered the ending.

The Zoom meeting was in twenty minutes, and he still had no idea what this woman looked like. Or what she looked like thirty years ago when what she looked like was relevant to the project at hand. He opened the folder Timo had sent him. There were no dates on the individual files, only random sounding phrases and words: Margiela Doll Parts, McQueen Voss, Margiela/Kawakubo Shoulders, Meisel Asexual 1, etc. He opened a file entitled White Show Runway. That must be her, a lean figure with bony shoulders and a prominent collarbone, wearing what looked like a torn slip dress that flowed over white slacks and white ankle boots. Some combination of the clothing and hair suggested the early aughts: he could almost hear Portishead in the background, nobody loves me like you do. On a closer look, he noticed two different top garments: a longer lacy robe covering a clingy chemise—both whitest of white, both with asymmetrical cut-outs and ribbons—with embellishments that, while disproportionate and unbalanced, were obviously carefully intentioned. She seemed tall, but her figure was isolated by a spotlight with nothing to provide scale. Her face was long, as was her neck, and the clothes fell off her shoulders impeccably, as they were designed to do. The lighting gave her skin a warm ivory shade, which contrasted with the white flowing material. Her expression wasn't blank exactly; it was neutral, disengaged, aware but not involved, not inviting, certainly not repelling, but deflecting. All models had that face. Most models had that silhouette.

He looked closer. Her thin chocolate brows formed a straight line, as did her thinner pale pink lips. Her black shoulder length hair was mostly in shadow. Her eyes were unremarkable: in this photo, they were dark, with any hint of color obscured. She was pretty, yes, in that symmetrical, composed way, but not extraordinarily so. Perhaps there was the smallest hint of a smile, indicating a propensity toward bemusement rather than contempt. He hoped there was something, some quality or attribute she possessed that he could use to avoid the clichés he feared would dominate, corrupting whatever prose he could conjure, spoiling any possibility of genuine effect. She looked so goddamned typical. Maybe that was the point. And he couldn't get that Portishead song out of his head.

He quickly opened another file, Garcons Lilith. It was a grainy ten second video of Millie on the runway, pink hair piled high, walking toward the camera. She was dressed entirely in black. There was no sound. He ran the clip eight or nine times. The scene started with a full-length shot, which quickly dissolved into a medium-full, then zoomed in further to a close-up before she began to turn and the clip stopped. It was difficult to see the clothes: they were black, as was the background. The tech was not sensitive enough to capture much detail, and the videographer hurriedly zoomed into Millie's face, as if that was where the interest lay.

What was she thinking here? Anything?

What was he thinking here? Anything?

The file was undated, but she couldn't be more than twenty-five here, more like twenty-one or two. Nineteen ninety-two or so. What was he doing in ninety-two? First year of grad school, drinking at Beirut with Timo, trying to sleep with, what was her name, they called her the sultry one? He couldn't remember. He did remember all attempts were rebuffed. Who did he sleep with that year? That girl from Aesthetics with the funny haircut? Jennifer something. Was that ninety-two or the year after? He pictured her sitting next to Timo near a blackboard. It must have been ninety-two. She had these feathered bangs and really red lipstick. She made amazing hot curries. Jennifer. . . Jennifer. . . Jennifer Morgan? Jennifer McGuire? Jennifer Morgan. Who was the sultry one?

He ran and froze the clip again and again, studying the different stills. From the full-shot, it appeared she was wearing some sort of sleeveless smock with black stockings and grey flats, pale arms dramatically framing the black flowing fabric. He found a medium-shot where her torso was illuminated by a camera flash that showed the smock was actually a double-breasted tunic with two rows of large, black buttons and barely discernible epaulets on the sleeves. He wasn't sure what any of that meant.

On the one hand, he was to be paid four thousand dollars, which was more money than he had ever directly made for writing in his life. There was the possibility of further work for Timo, who knew everyone, including those with money. And perhaps the glamorous world of international fashion would be a glittering change from his soul-crushing academic treadmill, which no longer had even the enticement of the city to mitigate or to recommend. His wife had encouraged his participation and insisted that if offered something similar, she'd be on it in a second. He'd heard the slightest threat in her encouragement and wondered to what temptation of her own she was referring.

But all that was before the disease, before the language became *unheimlich*—with words like intubation, social distancing, shedding virus, flattening the curve—and the comprehensive existential threat became manifest. Even if these weren't the end times of civilization (and he didn't believe they were, the Big Orange Buffoon notwithstanding), it did seem somehow authentically inappropriate, nihilistic even, to focus energy, time and talent on something as trivial and wasteful as fashion and its various industries (not to mention fashion and its industries of at least twenty years prior).

Plus, he would have to do some research. He'd have to look up this Margiela, as well as the other designers, talk to Timo, talk to his Sally, blah blah blah: the very thought of such study made him yawn. He had about ten minutes, time to get his rig set up in his office, arrange the books in the background, put on his professor face. He'd keep the photos up on his laptop for reference.

His phone rang. Timo.

Hey.

What's up? You get the photos I sent over?

Yep.

You take a look?

Yep.

Whenever you're monosyllabic, it means something's wrong.

This isn't my world.

No. But you can write. You'll have to use your imagination. I have some news, not sure whether good or bad. Our meeting will be a teleconference, not a Zoom meeting. It seems our heroine is stuck in Venice, and the bandwidth there is suss, or her computer's in Paris, or something, so you don't even have to put on a shirt.

I shaved for this.

That I doubt. Also, I can't make it. I got this thing that I can't get out of. So, it'll just be the two of you.

I'm not sure that's a good idea. Can't we postpone?

I sent her a long email: I'd just be repeating myself.

She's going to have questions.

Tell her to read the email. I'll try to join at the end, but no promises.

No promises here either.

Pour yourself a coffee and be your charming self. Fuck, I got another call.

So do I. It could be her. Six minutes early.

Off we go then. Cheers.

Wait, wait. Fuck.

Hello, hello? Are you there? Hello.

Hi, is this Millie? Millie Del'Aria?

Yes. Who is this?

Jonathan Dunn.

He got up and poured a cup of coffee and added cream, sugar. He stirred slowly.

Hello? Mr. Dunn? Is Timo on?

He sat down at the butcher block kitchen table.

Please call me Jonathan.

Where is Timo?

She had a deep voice, not breathy, but resonant. It somehow didn't fit with the photos he'd seen. Timo's not sure he can make it. He thought maybe you and I could have a conversation.

I don't know you.

He told me he sent you a substantial email. I assumed he provided some sort of introduction?

Yes. But I assumed I would be working with Timo as well. I don't know you.

I know Timo from way back. We went to grad school together.

She chuckled and then paused. He heard the slightest whoosh of breath. Was she smoking? Of course. Timo knows everyone, don't you think? But I do not. Know you. Why did Timo suggest you, do you have any idea? Are you a fashion journo?

No, I'm no fashion journo. I thought Timo explained.

He wrote that you had written books. He said you were *fidato, fidato* and *astuto*. He said you were a good writer. What books have you written?

I've written a monograph of the Countess di Castiglione, an Italian noblewoman who had over 700 photographic portraits taken. I've another book on Lee Miller and an article on Ghitta Carrell. And a chapter in a book on the Marchesa di Casati.

I know who Lee Miller is, but not the others. Is Ghitta a man or a woman?

A woman. Italian photographer in the 30s and 40s, he said too quickly. He took a sip of coffee.

There was a pause. He imagined her inhaling greedily, her cigarette pinched tightly between her forefinger and thumb. All of your books are about women—do you think that's unusual?

I don't know.

You don't know because you haven't considered it or you don't know because you haven't come up with an answer?

I've considered it. I don't think it's unusual.

Why, do you think?

Why what? Why have I considered it, why don't I think it's unusual or why have I written about these women?

Why have you only written about women?

I find the problems interesting: how do women live in this world? Was that a laugh? He stopped the next sentence in his throat. He was at a loss. His daughter, Addie, walked in through the hall door and opened the refrigerator. He got up from the table with his coffee, moved through the opposite door to the dining room and found the worn leather couch in the living room.

Timo had fucked up. This wasn't going to work.

At least the canals are clean.

Excuse me?

The water in the canals here, in Venice. You can see the bottom. There's no traffic—no *vaporetti*, gondolas, taxis, no tourists or anything—because of the lockdown. No one goes anywhere. So the water is clear. He heard some noise on the line. I'm looking for my cigarettes. Can you still hear me?

Yes.

Venice is completely abandoned. I walked from the Academy to Saint Mark's and didn't see a soul, except for some *carabinieri* who told me to go home.

Where do you live in Venice?

My friends have this place in *Dorsoduro*, near the Guggenheim. We were to meet up here a week and a half ago, but they're to remain in Zurich. I seem to be stuck here.

He spoke before he could stop: the Guggenheim was owned by the Marchesa di Casati, before Peggy Guggenheim bought it. She was known for her wild parties. She used to walk around with a cheetah.

My friends like to party. No cheetahs, not yet. I must say, I'm rather enjoying the solitude so far. Although the restaurants are closed.

He could feel whatever enthusiasm he may have once had for the project (and it was never very great) began to drain quickly from him. Her inner life, if she owned one, was likely little more than a series of clichés stacked one upon another. Stacked. He couldn't even think of an interesting metaphor.

It's very bad here. People are dying in Bergamo, Roma, Milan. You are in New York?

Upstate. The city got hit pretty hard, so we fled to Hudson.

I've been to Hudson. I would like to come back to New York, but I don't know when I'll be allowed.

He covered his mouth with his hand and half stifled a yawn. Immediately following this conversation, he'd text Timo and tell him he just couldn't do it, couldn't bear to record the banalities that would spill from those pursed lips and somehow form them into a coherent, vaguely compelling narrative. Even if he were to take up a more fragmented, associative approach, the likely superficiality of her memories would be the exact opposite of insightful or enchanting. Some, maybe even many, would find her triteness appealing—after all, fashion depended on the celebration of surface—but he didn't have to participate in this murder of intelligence by excreting still more cultural dross. He had promised, yes, and the money was good, yes, but he really didn't want to devote his time to such trivial pursuits while much of the world was coughing up blood.

So Timo is definitely not coming?

It appears not.

Can you explain to me, please, what we will be doing?

It should all be in the email. I don't know much more, only what Timo told me. It seems the new designer of Margiela, I don't remember his name. . .

Galliano. John Galliano. He's a creep.

Right, John Galliano. Anyway, this Galliano said something that got him into some trouble... He said he loved Hitler and that the Jewish women he was speaking to should be gassed.

Well anyway, he said something that got him into trouble and now he's trying to get back in good graces. So he's putting up money to publish a big Margiela retrospective catalogue. The museums wouldn't talk to him, but publishers, I suppose, are less picky and Taschen agreed to do it. Once Taschen agreed, Paris *Vogue* and the Belgian

Cultural Ministry came on board, so there's real money behind it. Margiela agreed to cooperate, but only on the condition that the book includes individual chapters on his collaborators: he mentioned you by name. So the editors are planning to devote a chapter to you, your career with and without Margiela. And I'm to write it.

A chapter on me. What on earth for?

He wants to include his collaborators, people who helped him and inspired his work.

He was a genius. I was never his muse.

You must have influenced him somehow.

We talked. I'd read to him sometimes. I was reading Tennessee Williams for some reason and Martin loved the way he sounded. We found a couple of the tapes and watched the movies. He liked Paul Newman. *Sweet Bird of Youth. Cat on a Hot Tin Roof.* I'm not sure how to make that into a book. Or if anyone would want to read it.

I think the overall plan is to include a number of photos with accompanying commentary: what you remember, what the clothes were like, what it was like to work with Margiela, what it was like to work with the other designers, other models, etc. Anything you'd like to include, anything you'd like to talk about, really. We could start with the important photos and work from there.

Why do I need a ghostwriter? And a man at that? Is the assumption I cannot write the story of my self myself?

No, I don't think that was the idea at all. I think they just want to use experts, professionals. Same way they

bring in professional hairdressers, makeup artists, photographers.

Are you a professional writer, then? You make a living from your writing?

He wondered if he could simply disconnect his phone, claim he had tech problems, and call it a day. Millie wouldn't mind, of that he was certain.

No, I don't make a living from my books. I teach as well.

Where?

SVA. School of the Visual Arts.

And what do you teach?

History of photography.

Are you teaching now, this semester?

We're teaching remotely. It's spring break this week.

But why you in particular? You're not a fashion journo. You don't teach fashion; you don't teach at FIT. Do I fit in to your series of distressed women?

Now it was his turn to guffaw. He wanted to say, if you are distressed, it's absolutely uninteresting. Instead, he said, you don't seem very distressed.

I am just curious as to what you want out of this.

I'm getting paid. And I want to stay in Timo's good graces. There might be other jobs down the road. He couldn't remember the last time he had participated in such an antagonistic conversation with someone he didn't know. He wanted very badly for this to end.

I understand the getting paid part. And I know how

helpful Timo can be. I'm just not sure I'm understanding your role in this. Or mine.

Timo insists it will be an important book, lots of photographs, a comprehensive retrospective of Margiela's work. Thick paper, quality reproductions, a lovely object.

Do you know Martin at all?

No, I've never met him.

Do you know his work? Either his clothing or his art?

I've been learning. Timo's sent some stuff, and I've looked at the videos of most of the shows.

You can get something out of the images, but seeing things on the internet is not the same as seeing things in person. The garments won't make much sense if you see them only from a screen.

We'll try to focus on you.

I was his fit model, his *mannequin de cabine*. Do you know what that means?

He said nothing.

I worked every day in the atelier. I was the three-dimensional body he tried his ideas on. I was the mannequin upon which he pinned, first the *toiles*, then the samples, then the quote unquote finished garments. It's incredibly tedious work, Mr. Dunn, standing still while he and or his assistants pinned, cut, corrected and adjusted, over and over and over. Then I'd walk toward him, walk away from him, walk faster, walk slower, turn around, turn the other way, sit, stand, kneel, twist, and then it would all begin again. Sometimes I could read, sometimes I couldn't.

Sometimes he'd help me with my French, sometimes it would be quiet all day. I certainly wouldn't call this inspiration, Mr. Dunn, nor collaboration. One might as well write a biography of a chunk of marble or a bolt of silk. I stood there, still, while he worked. And then I walked when he asked me to. I did this for six years.

But you walked in the shows.

Yes, and those were fun. But no one ever bought a Stockman dress because I wore it on the catwalk or a sheer flapper top because they liked my tits.

I'm not sure I understand you.

I'm not a supermodel. No one ever saw me; they saw the clothes. He could hear her take a long drag of her cigarette before the line quieted. You don't know the half of it.

I'm not quite getting this.

Yeah.

He looked at the picture on his computer. What about Hermès?

The H is silent.

Hermès.

Martin set that up. And I got paid. Saved my ass. What do you know about me?

Not much, just what I read on the internet.

What does it say?

He clicked to her Wikipedia page on his computer and read the first paragraph.

Jesus.

You've never read this before? That was a stupid question: her surprise and disgust sounded genuine.

After a few moments of silence, she said it doesn't look like Timo is going to join.

No, it doesn't.

I don't believe I will be able to help you, Mr. Dunn. As you know, I don't do that work any longer. I don't keep up with the people, the clothing, the industry. I don't think this book is designed to be up to date. I think everyone sees it as a retrospective celebration of Margiela's work, his career, his collaborations. I'm guessing they're still a year and a half until the thing is printed—probably more, given Covid—so there's no way it could be current. I think they want, I think *he* wants, different voices, different viewpoints and stories of what it was like to live and create the clothing and experiences you all did.

I don't care to relive, revisit or reclaim past experiences, mine or anyone else's. I'm sure you can find someone else.

I understand he was very specific in asking that your story be included.

I'm sorry.

Maybe Timo can change your mind.

Why do you say that?

Now it was his turn not to answer. Thank you for your time.

Goodbye, Mr. Dunn.

Goodbye.

Chapter 2
Alexander McQueen, "Voss"

At first glance…and in this case, is there ever a "first" glance? Isn't the glance here always determined by, dependent upon, other, previous, and subsequent glances? Isn't the point or punctum of each individual Castiglione photo created, at least in part, by the fact that our dear Countess, between the years 1856 and 1899, had over 700 photographic portraits taken?[7] Would we be looking at this image if it were singular, not part of an obsessive compulsive repetition? At "first glance," then, the photo *Elvira at the Cheval Glass* [figure 10] can be placed into two somewhat obvious registers: the photographic and the psychological (a decision of whether these registers are ever separate or distinct is partially the question under discussion).[8]

The photographic trope is one common to portrait photography: by using a reflective surface, one can simultaneously present multiple angles of the figure under scrutiny. The mirrored photographic image hints at a third dimension, a sculptural reality emerging from the flat two-dimensional magazine page or fine art print.

There is little that is new or revolutionary about this.

---

7 There has not been, to my knowledge, an exact count of the number of Countess' photographs. I have based my number on Abigail Solomon-Godeau, who, in her excellent "Legs of a Countess," bases her estimates on a collection by the Comte Robert de Montesquiou (over 400 prints); a collection of between and 250 and 350 negatives by Adolph Braun; and a late grouping once owned by the Gilman Paper Corporation. See Solomon-Godeau, "The Legs of a Countess," *October*, Winter, 1986 p. 70.

8 We must remember that Barthes' *Camera Lucida* hinges on a scene where he looks at a photograph of his recently deceased mother.

From the photos-with-mirrors used as early as 1850 (to document surgeries and other medical conditions and practices) to the 1861 insertion of an internal mirror into the camera mechanism itself (creating the Single Lens Reflex Camera) to the first mirrored selfie of the Grand Duchess Anastasia Nikolaevna in 1910 to the thirst-trap belfies of today, the use of reflective surfaces is a central or crucial technique in the history of photography's development. There is nothing evident in this photograph that either inaugurates or marks a particular advancement in the aesthetic or practice of portraiture, fine art or documentary picture taking. Unlike other photographs of the countess—like the shocking (for the time) images of her ankles and feet in *Study of Legs* [figure 4] or the poignant image of the sunken-faced *vieille folle of Tita Mina Blonde* [figure 23]—there is nothing provocative or even particularly memorable about this particular photograph. Anyone who has flipped through any fashion magazine in the past twenty years has come across similar, albeit more striking, imagery.

He was in his kitchen drinking coffee and desultorily reading an article on herd immunity when he heard his phone ping, and then a second or two later, a notification flashed on the top of his Macbook indicating an email message and a text. He reflexively opened the text and saw that Millie had invited him to a Zoom meeting. Millie the model? What could she possibly want?

He thought for a few seconds, then moved reluctantly to his study, where he'd set up his desktop Mac for his remote class meetings. He flicked on his ring light and clicked the email to open the program. He never liked his image on screen; his face always seemed pale, puffy and ill-defined. The camera angle was too low, and his chins dominated the frame. He adjusted his camera. Slightly better. His lumpy face still filled the frame: his eyes looked tired and his hair was messy. The unkempt academic. The distracted intellectual. He leaned back and buttoned his shirt. He joined the meeting.

Hello. Mr. Dunn? Are you there, Mr. Dunn?

Yes, hello. Millie? I didn't expect to hear from you again.

I can't see you. Can you see me?

No, the screen is black. Can you see me now?

Yes, yes, now I can see you.

He adjusted his screen back and forth. I can't see you. I can only see me, in half the screen. The rest of the screen is black.

She might have chuckled a bit. I can see you. Maybe we could just talk?

He leaned forward. Sure. It's strange not being able to see you. I feel at a disadvantage. Where are you calling from?

I'm in Paris, at the square *Georges Cain*. It is close to my flat. In *Le Marais*. Do you know Paris?

He imagined a light-filled park with well-dressed couples walking arm in arm. He watched as he shrugged his shoulders. I've been twice, but I don't know my way around.

It's nice today, not too hot. It feels good to be outside.

The background is mundane, non-descript. A wall of windows sits behind the ornately framed, slightly cantilevered mirror, extending from the center of the photo frame to the ceiling. Decorative wainscoting connects the windowed glass with a featureless floor. The wainscoting, depicting a columned balcony rail entwined with vines, draws attention away from the back of the dress, which is cloud-like and featureless save for its thickly scalloped hem.

We focus on the reflection of the model, the image in the mirror. This image, unlike the dress, is well-defined from the waist up, with a left arm crossing over her breasts and her right bent at a forty-five-degree angle at the elbow, the hand adjusting the high pleats of her pearl-dotted hair. A large, jeweled clasp, at least two bracelets, and a pearl necklace vie for attention, but it's the Countess' eyes, staring back into the mirror, that arrest our gaze.

The eyes, the eyes that stare into the mirror. . . what is she looking at? She is returning the gaze of the photographer, yes: she's looking at the photographer and, by extension, the viewer, you and me. Or she's looking at the viewer through the medium of the photographer. In any case, she's looking (back) at someone looking (back) at her. To be more precise, she's looking through a reflection to someone who is looking at her and her reflection. Or she's looking through a reflection to someone looking at an image of her and her reflection. In any case, she's looking at herself being looked at. She's not merely an object being viewed. Her return gaze marks a consciousness of being viewed: she is fully aware of her doubled (object and subject) position. In fact, she has done a great deal of work to compose this tableau in which she is viewed, in which she is viewed conscious of being viewed. She invites, insists, and enjoys being looked at. We know that without the photographs, the Countess would sink into the dustbin of obscurity and historical irrelevance. She knows it too.

How long have you been in Paris?

A couple of months. I was quarantined in Italy, in Venice, for a month. We spoke then. I've been in Paris almost two months. I had to stay in Italy for four weeks after we first spoke.

In the right half he could see his illuminated image, his face white and looming, dominating the window. He could see the light from the ring lamp reflecting off his glasses. The other side of the screen was black, save a vague reflection of the bookcase on the far edge. He imagined her, her long face shaded by a sun hat. He leaned back.

She didn't turn her camera off on purpose, did she? Would she? Didn't fashion models, people who made their mark in the world by being photographed, want to be seen? Pretending your camera wouldn't work, not even his students resorted to that. Well, they tried until he amended his syllabus. He couldn't imagine she would do that.

She is nothing (to us) if she is not seen. She exists to be looked at. The 700 photographs confirm this. This is the register that the Countess occupies: in her indefatigable insistence on being seen, she ostentatiously occupies the narcissistic position. Her gaze is the gaze of Narcissus.

He wondered what she was doing, wondered if the connection had broken.

On the one hand, this narcissism can be seen as a defense mechanism, a sublimation, a reaction to a society that was highly restrictive in the roles allowed women. Her physical beauty initially permitted Oldoini a social and psychological *existence*, a being-in-the-world primarily (perhaps almost exclusively) defined and determined by, dependent upon, the singular quality of corporeal loveliness. She had many lovers, but there was nothing else, as far as we can know, that she could do. She wrote letters, true, but she was no Madame de Sévigné. There were few women painters, photographers, composers or sculptors of the mid to late 19th Century, and little to suggest Oldoini was capable or even interested in pursuing any of those endeavors. She was a mother, a wife, and a mistress (reportedly of many, including Napoleon III and Victor Emmanuel II), but finally, these roles were impermanent and did not satisfy. She needed to be looked at. The photographs are documents, artifacts of that desire. At first glance, then, this is not a difficult narrative to construct.

If this worked as I'd hoped, you would see me holding up your book right now.

Oh? He was pleased. He leaned forward involuntarily, his head again filling the frame. Which one?

La Comtesse di Castiglione: Scherzo di Follia. I like the Italian title. I also like the photo on the cover.

That's a famous photo, where she's holding up the black frame around her eye. Striking. That's the image that got me interested in her.

It's a terrific cover.

He looked at himself on screen, leaning over, expectant, the bright image of his face contrasting strongly with the black half on the screen. He removed his glasses with his right hand and placed the tip of the temple in his mouth. Everything blurred. He waited.

He continued waiting. He wondered if the technology was interfering with their capacity to hold a passable conversation or if the pandemic and its accompanying forced solitude had perhaps dulled her social skills, or if she had ever possessed such skills in the first place. She could see him, could see that he was waiting, so why was she hesitating? Did she not know that the statement I read your book created the inviolable expectation that at least some elaboration, even the most perfunctory, would be offered, and to extend silence in its place was more than a violation of etiquette or insult but rather an omission that placed the speaker so far outside the pale as to render any further conversation impossible? What could be an appropriate response to such bizarre behavior? How long should he wait? He returned his eyeglasses to his face and looked at his image on screen.

Freud can be of great help here. From his classic text on Narcissism, we read:

We have discovered, especially clearly in people whose libidinal development has suffered some disturbance. . . that in their later choice of love-objects they have taken as a model not their mother but their own selves. They are plainly seeking themselves as a love-object, and are exhibiting a type of object-choice which must be termed 'narcissistic. . . With the onset of puberty, the maturing of the female sexual organs, which up till then have been in a condition of latency, seems to bring about an intensification of the original narcissism, and this is unfavourable to the development of a true object-choice with its accompanying sexual overvaluation. Women, especially if they grow up with good looks, develop a certain self-contentment which compensates them for the social restrictions that are imposed upon them in their choice of object. Strictly speaking, it is only themselves that such women love with an intensity comparable to that of the man's love for them. Nor does their need lie in the direction of loving, but of being loved; and the man who fulfils this condition is the one who finds favour with them. . .The importance of this type of woman for the erotic life of mankind is to be rated very high. Such women have the greatest fascination for men, not only for aesthetic reasons, since as a rule they are the most beautiful, but also because of a combination of interesting psychological factors. For it seems very evident that another person's narcissism has a great attraction for those who have renounced part of their own narcissism and are in search of object-love. The charm of a child lies to a great extent in his narcissism, his self-contentment and inaccessibility, just as does the charm of certain animals which seem not to concern themselves about us, such as cats and the large beasts of prey. Indeed, even great criminals and humorists, as they are represented in literature, compel our interest by the narcissistic consistency with which they manage to keep away from their ego anything that would diminish it (Freud, "On Narcissism," Standard Edition XIV, 88-89).

There is a lot to unpack here (some about narcissism, some about Freud), but again, the narrative of Oldoini's narcissism as a defense mechanism to her society's repression is an easy one to construct and to believe. The narcissist has attached all her desire to the self. We all do this to a certain extent (at least initially), but ideally, the healthy individual is one who can detach their interest from their selves and re-attach it onto their mother, onto an other, and eventually, of course, onto a more other other, a non-family member. During puberty, according to Freud's theory, the physical attractiveness of some women leads to an intensification of this original self-attachment, and all other attachments, all attachments to others, pale in strength and importance. This creates a 'feedback loop' of sorts: the subject begins to share the feelings of attraction others feel for her, and she becomes both the subject who desires (her self) and the object which is desired (by her self). This "self-contentment," as Freud phrases it, "compensates them for the social restrictions that are imposed." Others love her for her looks and detachment. She shares that love and becomes even more detached. The gaze the Countess returns to us in the mirror is a gaze of complicity: "Aren't I beautiful to look at?"

Did you like the book? He felt as if he was speaking to a child. He remembered a similar conversation, real or imagined, he had with his daughter after one of her first chapter books, something about James and an apple. It was hot, too hot to hold hands, and they were walking down a sidewalk somewhere, Brooklyn or Hudson, he wasn't sure.

Yes, I did.

It was a peach, not an apple. James and the large peach. Did you like the book? Why? What parts of the book did you like? What didn't you like?

I bought another book of yours, the one on Lee Miller.

Not a very exciting cover.

No. I just started it.

He studied his face on the computer. He tried to make his expression as blank as possible.

I like the first one. The brevity of the pause surprised him. Two sentences in a row.

Although I'm not sure I understand all the Freud. I mean I do understand it; I just don't agree.

Oh?

I don't believe that we're all governed by unconscious motivations. That makes the stories too easy.

That was partly my point as well.

I didn't get that.

Freud's a useful first step, but he's useful only as a first step. Much of his writing, his essay on Narcissism especially, is more about Freud than about his patients.

Do you think that all writing is narcissistic, Mr. Dunn?

What? No. He wasn't sure what she was getting at, although he could see where she might have a stake in arguing against the Comtesse's narcissism. I think writing is usually a way of asking questions: that's what the word essay originally meant, to attempt or to try. To try to understand.

You sound a bit defensive. He saw his brow furrow on the screen.

Freud goes on to argue that such sexual self-containment/contentment, like the narcissistic charm of toddlers or animals, is valuable and attractive. It is the attraction of the unknown (and perhaps unknowable), of the uninterested other, the other who does not desire us or who desires us only to the extent that we desire. Freud's clumsiness in expression can't quite mask his personal enchantment and fascination with the autonomous siren, whose seduction can be traced to the fact she is at once "the most beautiful" and blessed with "interesting psychological factors." What more could a man want?

But is narcissism ever completely, or even predominantly, self-contained? Freud thinks so, and the Greeks, up to a point, seem to agree. We remember that in the original story, Narcissus is largely a solo player, a handsome youth who falls for his reflection in a pool. In popular culture, however, and psychiatric thinking today, narcissism is defined not as a self-contained individual phenomenon but as a web of necessary and often destructive relationships with others. One need only look at the number of pop-psych books on narcissism to see that it has become a trope of (often damaging) relationships with others, not as a figure of self-containment, self-sufficiency or self-love. *The Diagnostic and Statistical Manual of Mental Disorders V* defines Narcissism as Narcissistic Personality Disorder. Here are three of the six listed criteria:

Identity: Excessive reference to others for self-definition and self-esteem regulation. . . Self-direction: Goal setting based on gaining approval from others. . . Attention seeking (an aspect of Antagonism): excessive efforts to attract and be the focus of others; admiration seeking (*DSM-V*, 767-68).

We see that narcissism in the contemporary mind is certainly different than either the young Hellenic beauty alone in the woods enchanted with his reflection in the pool (perhaps the literal origin of 'thirst-trap') or the beautiful siren of Freud, insouciantly sauntering through the captivated crowd. In today's world, the narcissist exhibits "excessive reference to others" for his "self-definition." His very existence depends upon others, upon the admiration and attention of others—there is no narcissistic self separate from the other. In some sense, this is a matter of degree, as in the definition above, the word "excessive" does a great deal of the heavy lifting. We are all primarily social animals; we rely on our relationship with others to define our being-in-the-world. Narcissists take this a step or two (or even three) further, as their existence independent of others' attention seems fragile and threatened.

I don't think I've ever written about myself. I don't have much in common with the Comtesse di Castiglione, the Marquisa de Casati, or Lee Miller. I was trying to think of Castiglione not in terms of narcissism but of self-consciousness. He could hear his professorial big-voice begin to emerge, so he leaned back. The difference is important.

I'm sorry, I didn't hear what you said.

The difference is essential.

I'm not so sure of the difference. Self-consciousness is a funny thing. I don't see it as a goal; it's more often a curse. I'm guessing the Comtesse was self-conscious from the beginning, whether she wanted to be or not.

Where did that come from, he wondered.

Anyway, you're right about the photographs being fascinating: I looked at them for hours. And how much trouble she must have taken. All those elaborate dresses and jewelry and hairstyles and props—my God. And the photography wasn't instant, so they probably couldn't see anything until they printed the negative. Or whatever they did.

She would probably have to hold the pose for a couple

of seconds at least. I haven't seen any of the negatives, but I bet there are some spoiled where she moved too quickly.

I like the ones she painted, like that blue and white ball gown. The one with that huge cage crinoline, where that overskirt basically engulfs that poor chair. I can't tell if it's got a seamed waist or not.

She had a professional paint the more intricate ones. You can tell the prints she did, they're much less detailed and messier: she was never adept at coloring within the lines.

That dress must have taken an hour to put on. I can't tell if she's wearing a corset—she likes that pose where she leans forward and her arms hide her waist; she repeats it a lot. She's not very old here, right, so her boobs probably didn't need much help. She does fancy her shoulders though. Until she got older. I can't believe it was just her and the photographer. She must have had someone to help her dress, fix her hair, her face.

It is obvious to see that the Comtesse di Castiglione fits this description to a 't.' In order to create the 'perfect shot,' the flawless memento (and testament) to her flawless beauty, she took a great deal of (self) care: she journeyed to the studio with trunks of dresses, costumes and other props; she meticulously dressed, groomed and posed herself again and again; she paid for the expensive society photographer; and she often hand-painted the resulting print. She played nearly every role—model, stylist, makeup artist, post-production editor—and she did so with the full knowledge of the aim of her activities: she wanted, needed, to be looked at. She did this over seven hundred times, the very definition of "excessive." And her gaze into the mirror tells us she knew exactly what she was doing.

Again, this narrative is difficult to dispute. A beautiful Italian countess of the 19th Century, lacking any alternative creative outlet or means to create/preserve her identity, takes to creating a series of elaborate and theatrical photographs taken by one of the pre-eminent Parisian society photographers as a testament to her beauty.

However, as seductive as this story may seem, I do have some questions. First of all, it is significant that the Countess did almost nothing to circulate the photos. She gave away some to friends, but for the most part, these photographs were seen by few, with most presumably viewed by only herself and Pierson. There is one hazy possibility of a single portrait photograph offered for public exhibition, and that was in a collection of Pierson's studio work in the *Exhibition Universelle* of 1867.[9] This simply doesn't fit with our post-Freudian understanding of narcissism. What narcissist would go to all that trouble, would wear the heavy and sumptuous costumes, would extravagantly style her hair and apply the elaborate and dramatic makeup to her face, would pose in sometimes difficult and provocative (and original) positions, and often would even paint and color the finished print, and then show it. . . to no one? This is self-creation at its most extreme (pure): to cre-

9 "The Model and the Photographer," *La Divine Comtesse* 44.

ate the self exclusively for the self. Far from today's Instagram tallying of likes, dislikes, follows, flames and peaches, Oldoini didn't seem to require or even consider the existence of an external audience, let alone its quantity. The photographs seem to be primarily, if not exclusively, for an audience of one: herself.

The studio kept records of its visitors, and they would write down if servants or other service people accompanied the sitter. I'm not saying these records were infallible, but there was never any indication that she brought along an entourage.

Even if she had help, I guess they would be her servants. The photographer, Peirson, what's his other work like?

Extremely traditional. He was the court photographer to the Second Empire in France, and took portraits of the Kings of Sweden, Portugal, Bonaparte the III. He was no Man Ray.

So this is all her, her vision. Were they lovers?

Nothing to indicate that they were.

Strange, strange. I can't imagine any photographer sitting back and letting the model make decisions. Every photographer I've known has been Charles in Charge: chin up arm back hips forward more not so much look sexy less sex eyebrow up less less more more quarter of an inch unbutton the top no button it again smile not so much more turn your toes adjust your elbow lick your lips

. . . I can't imagine any photographer just setting up his camera, adjusting the lights and then waiting quietly for the model to get dressed, fix her hair and face, arrange the props, find the pose and then indicate he should snap the shutter or whatever they did back then, no way.

She was his client: she paid for the sittings.

This by no means fits the contemporary definition of narcissism. But how does it do with the Greco-Roman (Conon, Ovid and others) and Freudian definition? There are, of course, significant differences between the ancient myths and the psychoanalytic, three of which we will need to mention. First of all, there is the unmistakable difference in the genders of the two subjects under discussion: male for the Greeks, female for Freud (the DSM suggests that between 50 to 75% of those classified as having Narcissistic Personality Disorder are male [671]). Secondly, with the Greek and Greco-Roman versions, Narcissus' gaze is instigated by his rejection of subjects who desire him, namely Echo and/or Ameinias. It is only after the rejection of these others that Narcissus views and falls in love with his own image. There is also, it must be remembered, the intervention of the god Nemesis in both traditions. Freud's narcissism is not founded on the active rejection or the intervention of the other but rather on the failure to move from the focus on the self to the focus on an external object—i.e., the mother. There is no third or even second party to the Freudian intervention; there is no other to reject or to seduce; there is only, always, finally, the self.

And perhaps the most suggestive difference between the Greek and the Freudian is the attitude of society toward the narcissist: while Freud finds the narcissist fascinating and almost necessary "for the erotic life of mankind," the Greco-Roman tradition is less sympathetic. Ovid writes, "Fool, why try to catch a fleeting image, in vain? What you search for is nowhere: turning away, what you love is lost!" (Ovid, *Metamorphosis*, trans. A S Kline, BK III 436). Pausanias is no kinder: "But it is utter stupidity to imagine that a man old enough to fall in love was incapable of distinguishing a man from a man's reflection."

And only the two of them? I've never been on a shoot with only two people. Usually there were ten or so. One of the Hermès spots I did, I think it was with Steven, there must have been twenty or so assistants, stylists, assistant stylists, art directors and their assistants, hair and make-up people, their assistants, two or three people from Hermès, everybody but Martin. Even the look books I've done always had three of four people. I can't imagine being alone with the photographer. One on one with Terry Richardson? No thanks. Have you ever been on a shoot? They can be wild.

No. Just no. He really wanted to avoid the interminable flatness of the louche Ibiza tale replete with superyachts, ecstasy and c-list genitalia. He wondered if she was trying to impress with her life-of-a-model anecdotes or if she was genuinely puzzled by the fact that the Comtesse seemed to be directing the production of her own images. For every positive reaction Millie inspired—and he was genuinely pleased she had read one of his books—she would, in turn, provoke a negative sentiment—in this case a more than slight resentment of her glamourous life. This negative sentiment didn't cancel out the positive but coexisted with it in a sweet and noxious cloud of staggering ambivalence. If she had called, Zoomed, whatever, only to discuss his books, that wouldn't be much of a problem, as he likely would have so little future contact with her that her effect on him would be virtually null. He was fairly certain, however, that she had contacted him in order to restart the Taschen project, which meant they would have to work together, which meant he would have to listen to her stories, which meant not only would he have to hear more of those glamorous unthinking insipid anecdotes, but that he'd have to try to fashion those small-minded Beautiful Women Syndrome memories into something vaguely approaching compelling. Or at least faintly interesting.

Where do Virginia Oldoini and her photographs fit into these sometimes opposing definitions? She is not today's influencer, thirstily calculating platformed views. Is she the beautiful youth, destructively enthralled with her own reflection? She is neither a youth nor destructive—if anything, her photographs are a record of her self creation, not destruction. Is she Freud's *femme fatale*, breezily and carelessly focusing the sexual vitality of a civilization? Her indifference is genuine and complete, not directed at any other, and not primarily (or even secondarily) a performance (genuine or not) directed at a male gaze. If the Countess' various self-contained photographs and poses appear somewhat close to the Freudian definition of narcissistic, I would argue that this proximity is actually superfluous or accidental. Although sometimes suggestive or even provocative (to the *Belle Epoque* eye), the photographs' power lies neither in their charm nor seduction but in their indefatigable *repetition* that moves their project from seduction to creation.

To put this another way, the question of whether the Comtesse di Castiglione's photographs are documents of a narcissistic personality is perhaps the wrong question. By focusing on this psychological definition, we perhaps miss the more authentic and philosophical question, that of self-consciousness. But for this, we will need more photographs and another chapter.

He wondered when she would bring the project up. He was determined not to make it easy for her. Timo had mentioned just a few days before that the overall Margiela project was still a go, although everyone was waiting for the vaccines and for the ability to travel and meet face to face. Without Millie's participation, he was in limbo as they had writers lined up for the other chapters, and no other model or secondary figure to replace her.

She was quiet, almost as if she had read his thoughts. Maybe she had changed her mind again. He wasn't terribly adept at making nice—his students often complained about this—and his expression may have betrayed his indifference. He felt a vague but undeniable disappointment at his disinterest in working with her, in working with someone whose life experience was so different and certainly more glamorous compared to his. But the last thing he currently needed was any gnawing reminder of his own beige existence, an existence bereft of any experience of Ibiza or c-list genitalia. He wanted to avoid reminders of the possibilities his choices had negated, the good drugs, tanned thighs and briny air he'd imagined in his youth.

Finally. I called, Mr. Dunn, to talk about Martin's project.

I wouldn't call it Martin's project. I don't believe he has editorial control.

I misspoke. About the project on Martin and his work, then.

As far as I know, it's still moving along. Since you told us no, I'm not sure what Plan B was or is. But as far as I know, no one's pulled the plug on the money—we're all just waiting to see what the winter will bring, pandemically speaking.

I talked to the person with whom I talk to about such things—I hesitate to use the word agent—and she convinced me that this might be, what was the word she used, appropriate, yes, that was it, appropriate to be included in such a project. You should be proud, she told me, of having been a central part of some very important artistic work, and while I am not convinced I was a central piece, I am gratified to have been involved in Martin Margiela's atelier during those years. So yes, I will be pleased to do what I can to honor him.

OK. I'll need to check with Timo.

He sent me your books, Mr. Dunn.

Excuse me.

Timo sent me your books. I was not interested. As I said in our earlier conversation, I detest nostalgia in general, Mr. Dunn, and for my own, I hold a particular distrust.

I'm not interested in nostalgia either.

Most men are, don't you think? Anyway, Timo asked me to reconsider and then sent your books along to me in Venice. I do like to read, and was alone and quarantined, and so I found them compelling.

So, my books changed your mind?

No. Martin texted and asked me to do it. That changed my mind. Your writing did convince me of your competence, Mr. Dunn. Your sentences show care and intelligence. I must say, however, that they also give pause.

Oh?

The women you've written about are dead, Mr. Dunn. I, as you will see, am not. There is a difference.

No argument here.

There will be arguments. I don't mean to be portentous, as this is not terribly important to anyone, but as I am not clear as to what it is you want, I am not clear as to what will disappoint.

I'm not sure what you want either.

And I can't imagine how you will react to such disappointment.

I don't know what to say to that.

I do hope you will be well paid.

Thank you, I guess.

We will be in touch then, Mr. Dunn.

I suppose we will.

Goodbye. She severed the connection.

Goodbye.

He stared at his image on screen. What did she see, looking at him? He imagined she was used to men, and women too, looking at her, so what did she see when she looked back? Or rather didn't look back, but just looked? Looked without being seen?

He couldn't see himself as she would see him; of course not. He never found his face particularly handsome, and with middle age, less so. He had kind eyes, he believed, but the lenses of his eyes glasses largely obscured them. The camera angle now hid his second chin but focused on his expansive forehead. His hairline had always been high and he needed a haircut.

Chapter 3
Martin Margiela, "The Red Show"

Is that her? The fashion model you're working with? Millie something?

Millie Del'Aria. That's her.

She's pretty.

I don't know. She looks like a model.

Most people think that's a good thing.

She seems elongated. Stretched out. Look here. Or here. See how she's almost perfectly vertical, linear? She looks like a Thomas Struth figure. These all look so nineties as well. Early nineties.

You like this body type: long and lean, minimal curves, gender indifferent. Do you remember what I was wearing when we met?

Of course. A tuxedo. With heels.

A Tom Ford Gucci tux.

Is that supposed to mean something?

With T-strap Prada pumps. Do you remember what you were wearing?

Do you?

Black docs black tee black Levi's.

That's what I always wore.

And...

And?

If it were just the black-on-black, we wouldn't be talking right now. What else were you wearing? Remember?

It wasn't my black Patti Smith shirt, was it? Or my Monica Vitti long sleeve? Although that was dark blue.

Nope.

No clue. Oh wait, my eyeliner. Right? And mascara? My sultry bedroom eyes.

Ha ha. It wasn't your guyliner. You overdid it.

What do you mean?

On a scale of Bergman to Caligari, you were somewhere close to a drunk Eva Green.

You never said anything.

Mmm.

If it wasn't my eyeliner or my monochrome outfit, it must have been my witty repartee.

Um, no. You were in a Diane Arbus phase at the time, if memory serves. And while I understood the attraction, the enthusiasm didn't really translate to seduction, appeal, or even mild curiosity. You were nervous and talked at me. At least at the beginning.

I'm a loser, baby, so why don't you kill me? Why did you take me home then? You must have been desperate.

You really don't remember? I'll give you a hint: *Und der Haifisch, der hat Zähne. Und die trägt er im Gesicht.*

What? Mack the Knife?

Der Haifisch. The Shark.

Still not following.

That jacket. That beautiful copper sharkskin jacket. With the turquoise lining.

I loved that jacket. My sister got it in a vintage store in Iowa someplace.

It made you look dashing.

I used to save it for special occasions. I was afraid I'd wear it out.

Whatever happened to it? Did you lose it somewhere?

I bent down awkwardly to pick up a toy or something at your dad's house, and the right shoulder seam ripped. I was embarrassed, hid it in some closet, and by the time I checked a couple of years later, it was gone.

Why were you embarrassed?

I was drinking.

Oh right. You should have told me. I'm sure it got tossed, alas. I wondered what had happened to it.

But that was it? That jacket? That's what attracted you?

Yep.

I mean, really? If I wasn't wearing that jacket that night, we might not be together?

No, it was all kismet. Take my hand, I'm a stranger in paradise.

I'm trying to be serious. At least somewhat.

Oh please. You, of all people, know details are important. You got annoyed by a few stray threads on my raw-seamed cropped jeans the other day.

They looked unfinished.

And how many times have you mentioned Helen Mirren's thick ankles?

I find her unattractive for other reasons.

I'm sure she's crushed. Yeah, your sharkskin jacket, it did catch my eye. It made it seem like you possessed some sense of the visual and wanted to stand out somewhat from your Columbia crit crowd and gave at least a small fuck about how you looked. That particular night, it was enough. Enough to have me walk over to the bar and say hi.

I had no idea.

And I wasn't desperate, far from it. I was still seeing Josh, although looking for exfiltration, to be honest.

So that's what I was, an escape clause.

Pretty much. At least that night. That's a nice picture. She's got long legs.

Her feet are gigantic.

Give me a break. She looks hot.

Thirty years ago.

I do not miss those thin eyebrows. Anyway, I think you protest too much.

I've not met her in person.

In the flesh, as it were.

We don't get along on the phone. Although she did read my Castiglione book.

There you go. When are you supposed to meet her?

Day after tomorrow. Down in the city. Not sure I'm going to go.

Why not? You could use the excursion. And we could use the money.

I don't feel like taking that fucking train. And the city makes me nervous, all those mouth-breathers. Last thing I need is to get sick.

Jesus, I wish I had an excuse to get out of the house. I'd go anywhere. . . city, country, suburbs, you name it. You should go, you could use something shiny. You're staying at the flat, make sure it's OK.

I'm not convinced about this project.

It'll be fun.

It won't be fun.

Well, you should go anyway. Sitting in front of a screen, looking at photos, it's kind of an old man's game.

What? How so?

Never mind. You should go. Get out of the house.

Haven't decided yet. I might just sit here in my underwear and leer at the purty girl.

Suit yourself. I'll leave you to it.

He clicked on another thumbnail. Millie sat on an old ratty car seat, her legs slightly spread, her left hand and skirt in front of her crotch. The dress, chair, alley floor and far wall were variations of green, changing gradually from the seafoam floor to the mint dress and slightly darker chair, and finally to the tea green mottled wall behind. Her shins and feet were foregrounded, dominating the fame with strong white verticals. Her crotch, shielded by her hands and skirt, centered the photo. Her hair was black, her face rouged and powdered, her eyes focusing stage right.

Her opened legs were somewhat inviting, although it took some work, thought, effort, to imagine himself, his college self, kneeling before her, his hands gripping her thighs, his face bending down to where her long legs met. Was this desire? Is that what he wanted, to eat her pussy and then fuck her on the green car seat in the green alley? If not, what did he want? He felt his dick stir ever so slightly.

The sucking and licking and fucking were part of it, OK, but what else? He clicked rapidly through other photos, each image covering three-quarters of the previous, advancing like a staircase down his monitor. Millie in color, Millie in black and white, Millie on the beach and Millie at the Parthenon, Millie on the darkened catwalk and Millie in the snow. Close-up red hair ablaze with diamond choker, medium-profile with stiff blue collar and black bangs, full-shot in multi-colored sweater, hair blonde and teased, close-up with shaved head, eyebrows covered with electrical tape and heavy kohl eyes. Catwalk video, glossy mag silhouette, grainy playground shot holding hands with a child. The accretion of images amplified her sexuality; the multiplicity awakened, if not lust, then certainly a vague ache, impassive and surprising.

Even with all the various facial configurations, poses, costumes, hair arrangements, settings and photographic effects—all her various 'looks'—there were consistent and recognizable details common to all the different images and scenarios. Her lips were always thickly colored, even when the rest of her face was natural or only lightly enhanced. Her feet were large, as he mentioned to Sally, and were seldom visible. She seemed to stoop slightly when relaxed, and her breasts were small and often difficult to discern, sometimes appearing as mere folds in the fabric. There was a full frontal black and white nude (Paolo Roversi), overexposed to highlight the inky pixie cut on her head and matching void of her pubic hair that centered the frame. She stood rigid, posed, her right hip jutting out, her torso twisting backward into the whiteness. The image reminded one of Tsuguhura Foujita's "Reclining Nude." The lush and ostentatious growth between her legs slightly shocked, as it seemed to contradict the carefully polished and groomed androgyny of so many of her poses. He thought such growth might be impractical, given how many times she would have to change clothes. Perhaps that was her little *taweez,* her secret resistance to the incessant tidying and airbrushing of her outward existence.

He clicked through other photographs and wondered if she wore unshaven pubes throughout. Here, in a strapless gown with impossible heels on a rain-slick street, or here, in a sleeveless dress on a well-lit catwalk, or here, with extremely low-cut denim jeans and a matching cropped vest. Her hair was often carefully unkempt and seldom more than shoulder length. Her eyebrows were always thin, sometimes nearly invisible, and all other hair, facial and auxiliary, was completely absent. He found a beach shot, tomato red skirt with matching two-piece top, and zoomed in, looking closely. Pure skin, unblemished and smooth. She was young here, granted, but such depilatory perfection post pubarche was cultural rather than natural: hence, perhaps, the luxurious concealed minge as a private reminder of the possibilities of freedom.

This was an angle, a possible hook, a way of rounding her off into a viably interesting character by assigning some depth to her ubiquitous superficiality: the young, beautiful American from the high western plains, plucked onto the Parisian catwalks, ostensibly civilized but untamed beneath the glad rags and threaded brows of European couture. Was that too cliché? Was it possible to be too cliché in fashion? The beauty and the bush.

He had always found fucking women he was intellectually invested in more satisfying than sex with randos. Not that he was necessarily averse to one-night stands, but his libido had always been stimmed by a well-turned phrase or pithy retort as much as a toned ass or a delicate ankle. His marriage was indisputable proof of that. But did unshaven pubes really indicate intellectual depth or a sophisticated imagination?

The fact that she had read his book was perhaps proof. It was natural to him, in a clever and artistic way, to somehow associate that intellectual activity with her magnificent tuft of pubic hair in order to create a creature of necessary (he thought) depth and complexity. This was a way of making her story more complicated, more alluring.

But there was something else, something perhaps approached by the term glamour. He wished he could think of another word, but that was the best he could come up with. There was perhaps some magic, some pixie dust, some quality outside the features he could index and catalogue. He opened another file, Hermès Elle. The screen was filled with a black and white close-up of her face rising over the peak of her right shoulder, her long neck stretched and turned so that her eyes met the camera full on. Her hair was short and black with soft bangs that accented her smoky eyes. Her brows were stylized, skinny and arched. A small, deeply golden bottle of Hermès *Calèche* drew his gaze to the right bottom corner, but he quickly looked back at her eyes. They were prominent in her face, more almond than round, and her irises floated above the horizon of her bottom eyelid. What was it called when you could see three whites of the eye? Some Japanese term he couldn't remember. Her left pupil was slightly elongated, almost teardrop shaped. Both pupils were extremely light, lighter than the skin of her cheeks and forehead. It was likely some photoshop adjustment or maybe contact lenses. The eyes were languorous, elegant. He wasn't sure why those two adjectives attached themselves to the image before him, as they were neither particularly insightful nor terribly apt. But there they were, near meaningless modifiers now stuck fast to the image he had of her grey spheres staring back at him, staring back at him unmistakably languorous and elegant.

Her mouth neither promised nor denied. Her darkened lipstick attempted to plump, but the shade could only partially mask the relative flatness of her lips, which formed a thin, perfect line, a line not of indifference but of reserve. The mouth seemed to negate the promise or suggestion of the eyes, not with ill intent, but with the caveat that further involvement was unlikely. She had a well-contoured philtrum, with two strong but terse lines between her nose and upper lip.

The photo was at least twenty years old. He wondered how her eyes had aged.

What did her eyes promise or lips suggest? Why did the not uncommon combination of lighting, camera angle, lens choice and filter, skin foundation, mascara and eye-shadow, facial bones and ophthalmological structure provoke a visceral reaction? It was for sex, maybe, but not only for sex: maybe there was some imaginative longing to be seen with her and her beauty the morning after, together, happy and smiling, enjoying a late Slim Aarons Capri breakfast. He had no difficulty picturing Millie, cigarette in one hand and croissant in the other, champagne bottle ready to hand, brilliant half smile beneath oversize black sunglasses and a lime green sun hat: he could imagine her quite easily. It was difficult to place himself in such a scene, however, as his sharkskin jacket would detract, and he now had zero tolerance for cigarette smoke.

But was that it? Was the erotic charge, such as it was, traceable to some sort of jolt to his imagination? The image of the morning after was not terribly original nor terribly heartfelt. He had thought there was something sinful—he couldn't escape that word despite its imprecision and the bourgie morality it marked—when first confronted with the fashion industry and this project, but Millie, somehow, didn't rise or sink to that level of transgression. She was too shallow for the Old Testament and too apathetic for the New. Her crimes were misdemeanors, the self-absorbed misbehaviors of thoughtless youth (of any age) who knew they would not soon die. Her beauty was intimidating, but it was the impersonal intimidation of those blinded by their own reflection. She was vain enough to remain genuinely ignorant of her beauty; by discounting what others found valuable, she managed to simultaneously ignore and denigrate their desire and taste.

This was ridiculous. He was spending far too much time constructing an elaborate narrative based merely upon a disembodied voice on the telephone and various manipulated and pixelated images on his computer. His assignment was a hack job, nothing more. He would look at some photos and would reread her Wikipedia page and anything else he could find on her after dinner and on the train, then meet with her and construct some story of her life. There was no need for any other involvement, be it emotional, intellectual or (pseudo-) sexual. There was nothing else he needed to understand. There was no need to construct a narrative of desire about a woman he'd never met based on photos from a lifetime ago, thirty years prior. Yes, she did read his book and yes, she did, at one time at least, sport a magnificent tuft of pubic hair. And yes, his wife thought she was shiny. So fucking what.

But he couldn't quite drop it. He had read somewhere that the demand for reproductive possibilities unconsciously determined sexual attraction: everyone, it seemed, had some sort of biological clock ticking somewhere in their gonads. Maybe Millie's allure could be traced to some genetic instinct to propagate the species with health and vigor. But look at her. With few exceptions, she appeared gaunt and almost spectral. Models were skinny, OK, but a severely honed shoulder blade or the coin purse collarbone couldn't lend itself to fantasies, cognizant or cellular, of procreative multiplicity. He could find nothing in the photos that suggested even the possibility of empathy. Nothing in her gaze, clothing or pose suggested that she would share anything: not a bed, an experience, a sandwich, or a child. Contact could be made, and situations could be separately enjoyed, but communion or even fleeting intimacy were out of the question.

Or maybe he was just projecting. Creating a narrative of cold detachment as a way of making her make some sense to him. He was deeply disappointed in the fact that all the appropriate narratives that came to mind seemed so limited and crimped. Either her image or his imagination was tired. Probably both. This *was* an old man's game. Why was he playing?

He leaned forward and looked in her eyes, all the while realizing the cliché. Clear, like windows. He very much preferred his previous justified irritation to the current possible attraction. Not that he was worried about any attraction being mutual—he entertained few misconceptions regarding his own essential pull—but did possess enough self-knowledge to know that he often acted differently (solicitous to the point of unctuousness) to women (never students, thank God) he found attractive. He would *not* act the fool in front of someone whose entire being (he supposed) was solely constructed to initiate such a response.

Cataloguing the individual details that combined to create her beauty was no problem. And that was all that the job required. There was nothing else he needed to understand. He did not need her to make his job more difficult; that was certain. He would meet with her, smile, listen to her stories, and write a few sentences he wouldn't feel ashamed of. And then get paid. He could do that.

Chapter 4
Martin Margiela, "The Stockman Show"

So, what's up?

Thought we could talk before Millie gets here. She usually on time?

In my experience, most fashion models are. There's always someone else to take their place. What's on your mind?

I don't think I can do this.

I can't get you any more money.

It's not the money. You read the news, yes? People are dying, cops are killing, and the planet's burning. People in the city, a few blocks from here, are starving.

We're on the Upper East Side.

And we're going to discuss hem length, detachable sleeves and a blouse made of gloves from thirty years ago? Too much bullshit.

This seems like your thing, though, right? Casati pissed through her entire fortune on parties, cheetahs, and absinthe, Castiglione burned through *her* entire fortune having her portrait taken like six hundred times, and Lee Miller loved those beauty-against-rubble shots of Lanvin gowns in bombed out theaters, the stocking seam just so against the splintered beams and shattered brick.

She was a war correspondent.

For *Vogue*.

She went to Dachau. To Buchenwald.

OK. Millie's no Lee Miller.

She went to Dachau and Buchenwald. She came home and couldn't take the bullshit. Tended to her garden and buried her past. Became a gourmet cook. It was her son who resurrected her career.

Still not seeing what that has to do with Millie. Or with you.

Doesn't it bother you in the least? We're not out of the pandemic yet. Remember the refrigeration trucks parked next to the morgue? California's burning, immigrants are downing, police continue to run amok. . . it's kind of hard to focus on the trivial.

Did you get your shot?

Of course I got my shot. I'm here, aren't I?

Pfizer or Moderna? Or J&J?

Pfizer.

Didn't you have it?

In October. Mild case. Three-day fever, bad sore throat for a week. Don't change the subject.

OK, the world sucks. It's usually sucked. About twenty million people died in World War One, not including the flu. About sixty million in WW Two. Covid 19's killed what, four million, five? So, if you want to crunch numbers, we're actually making progress.

Don't be a dick.

There were some great clothes during both wars. You ever see any Fortuny gowns? Exquisite.

You keep changing the subject.

I'm trying to provide the opportunity for you to avoid

speaking stupid. I see that you're going to insist. OK. The world sucks. How does you not working on Millie's book chapter change that?

I don't want anything to do with the whole shebang. Fashion is indefensible. The excess, the waste, the whole fucking cycle of buy, wear, ditch, repeat. The earth can't take it.

You're right. Fast fashion is unsustainable. But that's not what we're talking about. I doubt very seriously Millie shops Zara or H&M. You still haven't answered my question: what does your refusal have to do with all that?

Not to mention the damage it does to the self-image of thousands of women and girls who can never meet those impossible standards of female beauty.

You're not pissed at Millie or anything? She can be irritating.

No. We're not exactly best friends, but we could work together. Although her fake accent is annoying. But it's not about her. The whole fashion industry is morally bankrupt. Rich skinny white women paying thousands of dollars for clothes only they can afford or wear: an entire industry built on exclusion and conspicuous consumption. I don't want to be a part of it.

Bankrupt? Why the conflation of banking with morality?

So I'm the voice of puritan banking morality?

All morality is puritan banking morality. It's as if there is only so much time, money, energy in the world, and to spend it on fashion would mean that there's not enough to spend on other, more immediate concerns, like housing, food, water. . .

Social justice, climate mitigation. . .

Not only is there a whiff of the bank book in your discussion on morality, but there's also something of Savonarola in your thinking of aesthetics. And that's new. I can think of two reasons for your reluctance to work on the chapter. The first is that you can't take, or rather spend, the time. Given that the world is teetering on the precipice of absolute disaster—politically, economically, ecologically, and culturally, have I missed anything? —you need to devote your waking hours to activism and civic engagement. You need to organize, write petitions, knock on doors, and put your energy and intellect into working for social justice and climate rescue, and anything that might distract you is wasteful and or toxic and needs to be ignored. And if that were truly your reason, well, I would understand it. I wouldn't agree with it, but I would understand it.

But really, that ain't you. You teach photography studies, specializing in the decades between the 20s and 70s, work that you seldom connect to questions of racism, classism, sexism, or climate exploitation. I've yet to see you arrange or even attend any sort of viewing, panel discussion, seminar or lecture that might somehow be related to crises you mentioned earlier. I've never seen you at the Food Bank, and I can't imagine you raking plastic out of the Hudson or writing some exposé on the East Greenpoint Water District.

The second reason I can think of is more interesting. You believe that if you were to work on this fashion project, your moral integrity would be compromised.

Yes.

Oh dear. You know what this reminds me of, don't you?

No idea.

You're the priest of ressentiment.

Oh God no, no! I hated that fucking class.

All your talk of sin and morality, that's what it sounds like to me. Are you sure it's not because of Millie?

Millie hasn't triggered me if that's what you're suggesting. I've just never thought about the fashion industry until now.

Obviously.

And now that I have, well, let's just say I find it. . .

Hello.

There she is. Hello Millie. Jonathan and I were just talking about fashion.

Your shirt in particular?

Ha ha.

It took him just a few beats to recognize her—although the word recognize felt wrong because he had never met her before—in person, in the flesh, standing next to their table outside the tavern. Eventually he managed to reconcile (the 're' again) the details from her photographs—the sharpened cheekbones, the long neck, piercing blue eyes—with the features of the figure facing him. Part of the trouble could be traced to the ontological discrepancy in media between RL and screen, as well as the disparity in resolution, as the real-life silhouette was sharp and well-defined. The colors, too, were brighter and more liquid: her brilliant blue jacket—which sparkled with its own cerulean light—seemed to step out of one of those Eggleston Memphis prints. In addition, unlike the videos he watched, in which she moved awkwardly, acting with apparent astonishment at her corporeal embodiment, her gestures here were smooth and lissome, her smile animated, her eyes languorous and elegant.

That wine for everyone?

Let's get you a glass.

We were talking about fashion and morality. Or the lack thereof.

Morality? He's right. Most amoral bastards on the planet. Would sell their mother's soul for a front row at the Spring Summer Dior. It's all about the dollars, the do-re-mi. Morality in fashion: short fucking conversation.

Jonathan is feeling morally compromised by working on this project. And we're trying to find out why.

Good for him. We need more young idealists. Can I get a wine glass? Thank you.

It's not the individual people he objects to; it's the industry itself. Or not the industry, necessarily, but the whole enchilada, the entire spending-all-this-money-on-clothes-no-one-can-wear thing. We are fiddling while

Rome is burning, apparently.

Thank you for the glass. Since we're outside, can we smoke? No? Do you have any paper menus? I hate those things on my phone. . . Thank you so much.

All I said was that I'm not sure we, I'm not sure I, should be focusing so much energy trying to analyze the earth-shattering cultural phenomena of wearing a sweater made of old socks or boots with a slit separating the toes *from thirty years ago* while our planet seems to be going to hell in a handbasket. Maybe I shouldn't have used the word moral. But yeah, I do think there's something sketchy about it.

Maybe he's right, maybe we should shut the whole thing down, put on our Mao jackets and get to work.

Carhartt overalls.

In brown or beige.

Timo thinks I'm a priest of ressentiment.

Resentment?

No, the Nietzschean concept of ressentiment.

Perhaps we should save this discussion for another time.

Condescending much? What is this ressentiment?

Oh, dear. Where to begin? First of all, some think fashion is completely useless and superfluous. Clothing is a necessity, true, but fashionable clothing is based on such pointless and superficial details that it betrays its very function—to mask and to protect—so to spend any time or money on such vain and senseless minutia is an unnecessary indulgent expense. Jonathan used the term morally bankrupt, which suggests that this unjustified and frivolous expenditure has a moral aspect to it: it's not just bad business, it's bad acting, bad faith, bad consciousness. Evil.

Secondly, fashion speaks to only a limited number of human beings, those who can afford the clothes and those who can fit into the clothes. If we were to make a Venn diagram, the intersection between necessary body type and disposable income would be tiny indeed. So not only is fashion trivial, but it's also elitist.

Ressentiment contra couture.

Nietzsche believes ressentiment comes in two forms, or from two sources. There's the ressentiment that comes from the masses, from the slaves, as he calls them. This explains Trump, Brexit, the National Front in France. . .

Rassemblement National.

National ressentiment.

For Nietzsche, morality is basically a creation of the slaves when faced with desires they can't obtain. The masters, the noble, they are strong and have a will to power that allows them to satisfy their desires, including desires of self-knowledge. The weak or impotent, on the other hand, don't possess this will and so create rules and regulations to inhibit or constrain the masters. The noble being says Yes! Yes! to life, to appetite, to sex, beauty, knowledge and experience. Slave morality, morality as such, says No. And not only a personal or internal No but a social or cultural No. *Thou* shall not!

Will to power? I'm not sure I like that. It sounds like license for white guys to do whatever they want.

The ideal is that there should be no *external* restraint, no inhibition from outside, from others, from the weak, the stupid and the afraid.

Nietzsche was a fascist. And look where the will to power has gotten us today.

The problem today is that everyone, even the most mediocre, considers themselves an *ubermensch*.

What did Nietzsche have to say about that?

Not much.

In other words, you haven't sorted it yet.

In other words, I haven't sorted it yet.

So how am I a priest of ressentiment?

I'm getting to that. Anyway, it's slaves who want to become masters, so their moral No should be expected.

That's your insight? We need more wine.

More of the same?

Sure.

Here's my question: what is it that makes fashion immoral to people who should know better, i.e., the writer, the intellectual, the artist, the people Nietzsche calls priests? Is there a buried wound, some primordial and profound affront, that has stuck in the craw of writers and artists and created an unforgiving and all-encompassing moral judgment against fashion as a discipline or art-form?

Sexism.

Yeah. Fashion is women's work. It's not serious, not worth thinking about. Thank you, Virginia.

I can't see that. These are the 2020s. And much of the No to fashion comes from women and from, dare I say it, feminists.

Be careful. Both of you.

The No I'm talking about is more fundamental than the No of feminism. The No I'm talking about is negative on many different levels. One of the most fundamental problems of priestly ressentiment is that it says No to the self as well as to the other. We know that slaves can't create narrative. They can vaguely dream of a change of circumstance where the slave is now king, but the king/slave plotline remains fundamentally unchanged. They can even overthrow their kings, but because they lack the necessary imagination, their revolution always results in terror and bloodshed, and almost always results in an even more oppressive sequel than the original. The most ardent revolutionary, if he lacks imagination, becomes the most terrible tyrant. This, according to Nietzsche, explains the narrative of Christianity.

In the slave ressentiment, the only things negated are the positions of the slaves and masters, and the story remains the same. But the priest is more cunning than the slave, and so his ressentiment, his negation, is more complex.

It goes something like this. Here you are, Jonathan,

in your solid (more or less) middle-class life, comfortable but not too comfortable, a mild success in that you have a healthy nuclear family, can teach and study what you want, but not such a success that you don't feel either the tinge of professional failure and regret or the financial squeeze of upcoming college tuition and New York City prices. Into this mild existential ambivalence comes a glimpse into another life, a life of glamour and decadence, of physical beauty and metaphysical irresponsibility, a glossy sun-drenched Dionysian life of freedom, youth and sex. And it's not just a theoretical glimpse, no, it has a face, a real face of flesh and blood, a face present and unavoidable, a face that likely has become unforgettable. A face that is exactly the same age. A face that is, in some sense, a mirror image of what you are not.

Oh yes, I'm so fucking successful and happy. You don't know me at all, Timo.

I'm not talking about reality, Millie. I'm talking about what our friend Jonathan sees.

I can't decide if I should be insulted or embarrassed.

Perhaps I should stop.

Embarrassed for whom?

Go on.

Are you sure?

Please do.

And so you, Jonathan, say to yourself, I would love to be beautiful, rich, live in Paris and go to sexy fashion parties. I would love to have someone write a story about

me and my sexy fashion Parisian parties of yesterday so
that maybe I'll be invited to even more sexy fashion Parisian parties today. But, alas, my life has worked itself out
so that these things I desire are not likely to happen. In
truth, I realize there's not one thing I can actually do in
this world so that I could actually in this world attend one
of those sexy fashion Parisian parties. So, what do you do
with this frustration, with this knowledge that you will
never be able to reconcile your desires with your capability of achieving said desires? You construct a story, a
fictional narrative where values are inverted, where the
unreachable objects of your original desires are narrated
as worthless, insignificant and even immoral. You never
wanted any of these Parisian glamour parties in the first
place. You construct an elaborate narrative system, with
metaphors, figures of speech and "common sense" to tell
this story, to yourself as well as others, that the unobtain-
able Parisian glamour parties are, in fact, not worth the
trouble, that they are boring, indulgent and finally even
immoral.

Not sure I've done that.

It's not you, not only you. Your story fits seamlessly into
an elemental narrative already created by other priests of
ressentiment, the theology that applies the shopworn but
paradigmatic model of internal and external to human
beings, who now have an inside and an outside, a truth
and an appearance, with the internal privileged as trust-
worthy and profound and the external as superficial and

deceptive. There is the aforementioned economic component of this model, which insists that talents ascribed to one are balanced by a corresponding lack in the other: one can possess either beauty or brains, but not both. You fool yourself and others by saying that these Parisian glamour party experiences are worthless and immoral and that true beauty, true experience, is giving to others, for example, loving your neighbor, living for the community. If one is an academic, one says that fashion is superficial, that it has no deep, internal meaning, that it simply clothes and covers. To pay attention to fashion is thus an immature and/or criminal waste of time. Real value is found in the mind, in abstract thought and theory. If one is an artist, one insists that fashion does nothing to solidify the community, quite the opposite, and that it does not express universal truths that elevate the concepts of family, work, land and equality to supreme values. And because fashion doesn't do that, *voilà*, fashion is immoral.

I know what this has to do with.

What?

I know what you're on about. I know your original wound, Timo, what has stuck in your craw. This is about your dissertation, isn't it?

Probably.

What dissertation?

Do you want to tell her, or should I?

I will. You know, it doesn't change anything.

We are both priests of ressentiment.

What are you talking about?

We were at this party in graduate school, and I was talking to one of my professors, a man I admired tremendously. I was hoping to ask him to direct my dissertation. We were talking, and he asked me what I wanted to write on. When I told him fashion, he replied Oh really, German or Italian?

So?

He thought I said fascism. He never considered that anyone serious could write a dissertation on fashion. No one did. At least not back then.

I still think he was pulling your leg. He wanted to see how you'd react.

Maybe he did hear and was being literal.

Yeah, right. Lagerfeld or Gucci? Boss or Versace? I don't think so.

How did you react?

I found someone else to work with. I wrote a half-assed dissertation on Proust. And I vowed to create a life for myself outside of academia.

You've done pretty well for yourself outside of academia.

Have I?

You've been to those fancy Parisian glamour parties, I've seen you. You've been to the Met Gala.

I was working.

Two men, two priests of ressentiment. One believes in fashion, the other doesn't. Now what? Or rather so what?

Ressentiment is not a condition one should admire or cultivate. It's a condition to avoid.

Why?

Ressentiment is not imaginative; it's passive and negative. Moral judgments are negative admonitions for others—thou shall not—and they really don't offer any creative alternatives. When you said you didn't want to work on the book, you didn't have any idea of what you would do instead. It was just this vague No.

And when you said you wanted no part of academia, did you have an alternative career in mind?

The priest of ressentiment, his soul squints.

Is that you or Nietzsche?

Nietzsche. Ressentiment is sentimental, nostalgic, based on feelings of loss and inadequacy. It's a story of the eternal flashback, of the perpetual No, the incessant and omniscient inhibition of desire. There's no action or thought, just the impotent emoting of sadness and rage. It's first and finally a bad story. Bad, not in the sense of evil or malevolent, but in the sense of flawed and deformed.

There's more.

I'm not surprised.

Look at yourself in the mirror. I don't mean in any existential way, and I'm not trying to be insulting, but look at your personal fashion, your clothing decisions. What are you saying with your outfit, your look?

I'm not saying anything.

You know better than that.

I guess I'm saying I can't afford to pay $400 for a shirt.

This shirt costs half that.

Ok. I can't afford to pay $200 for a shirt.

I've seen you spend $200 on record albums easy. Your wife and I have given you some nice clothes. But you prefer your grad school black to the pale blue Armani shirt I gave you last year or that Tom Ford windowpane your wife gave you for Christmas. Today, meeting Millie, what did you choose? Underneath your forest green LL Bean jacket? Black Levi's, distressed, by you, not on purpose, a black polo from Uniqlo and black Chuck Taylor's with nameless black socks.

Maybe he's in the Crow tribe?

I'm sure you took some care today with these choices. What are you saying with them? You're saying the same thing almost all academics and writers say, and far too many artists: you are saying that you are too busy and too profound to spend much thought and energy on something as frivolous as clothing. You are saying that you are more serious than we are. More serious and more real.

This is what I often wear.

This is your uniform, right. Your look. Your look that says don't look at this look. Your look that says *I'm* the one who looks.

You're losing me.

I'm the one who judges.

All black, like a priest.

I'm the one who knows.

Should we get some food?

Wait a sec, wait. Look at this. There. What do you see?

What is it?

The model's name is Winnie Harlow. The designer is Iris Van Herpen. Do you find this dress beautiful?

Actually, I do. But I don't see how any woman could wear it, with all their floaty appendages, drifting headdresses and weightless flounces.

What about this one?

That's even better. It's absolutely stunning.

Van Herpen doesn't do *prêt à porter*, ready to wear, off the rack.

I know what *prêt à porter* means.

All of her clothing is *haute couture*, bespoke, made to order.

I get it.

Wealthy women go to Amsterdam to get dresses made for them. Actors. Brides. Without the wealth and power you find immoral, these dresses would not exist. Without the system of large money and a certain expensive taste, these garments would exist only as *croquis* on paper or a computer hard drive. Or in Van Herpen's head. Since our metaphors are financial, let's ask in these terms: is it worth it?

I have no idea how much money we are talking about.

You need a figure? $20,000? $200,000? $10,000? $5,000? What's the cutoff? At what price point does the beautiful move to the obscene?

That's not fair.

Where do you think Van Herpen's politics are? Do you think she's left wing, right wing, socialist, fascist, what?

I've no idea.

Neither do I. But these are beautiful, right? We are happy they are in the world. But the system that produces them, does it have a right to exist? Could we say it exists outside of morality? Beyond good and evil, as it were?

You think Van Herpen has a will to power?

A will to beauty. We possess art lest we perish from the truth.

Nietzsche. And Marc Jacobs. What about Chanel? Does she have a will to beauty, too? Show him photos of little black dresses. Or the suites. The Jackie-O.

She was a Nazi sympathizer.

Nazi spy. She used Aryan race laws to steal Chanel #5 from her Jewish business partners.

It was complicated.

Many of my friends won't wear Chanel, clothing or perfume. My friend, Yael Goldman, sewed yellow Stars of David on all her Chanel dresses. *Jude.* I should do that.

What about that guy, Galliano? The dude who's paying for all this? He's a neo-Nazi, right?

Touché.

It is complicated. Anyway, Millie's right; questions about dollar amounts aren't fair. And not really the point. We don't need to go to the extreme with Van Herpen and her $20,000 bridal gowns. Let me suggest that while fashion might not be moral, it is ethical. I'll say it again: fashion is ethical.

I don't know how you can possibly say this. Look at how fashion operates. It rigorously excludes what the current trend defines as being outside its incredibly narrow definition of beauty. And do we really want to detail the endless abuses of labor endemic to the industry? Do we really need to mention the sweatshops at home and abroad, the abused child workers, the slave-waged workforce? And to go up the chain a bit, how can the tremendous environmental damage fashion wrecks upon the earth be defined in any possible way as ethical? What are the ethics of producing a tremendous amount of greenhouse gases? Of polluting our oceans and streams with toxic dyes? You're not going to convince me that fashion is ethical. Nope. No way.

I'm not talking about fast fashion. I'm not talking about the means of production. I'm talking about fashion's aesthetics, if you will, its ontology.

You need to define your terms.

If morality is how others see us and determine our behavior, then ethics is about how we see the other as other. Do we try to make the other the same? Or do we genuinely respect the otherness of the other? If we can move from Nietzsche to Levinas, a rather quick move, I admit, we see that it is our ethical responsibility to let the other be. . . other. Which is extremely difficult. It requires—get ready for this—love.

I have no idea what this has to do with fashion.

Fashion's beauty, its peculiar beauty if you will, is its omnivorous inclusivity. Put simply, there is no object which cannot be made beautiful. Just as there are no wrong notes in jazz, only notes at the wrong places. I'm not talking about the past, nor am I necessarily talking about the current trend of ugly fashion, which really tests my theory. Look at this picture of Bella Hadid. See those grey herringbone hotpants, red Adidas sneakers and black knee socks. And the faux poison green rabbit fur stole around her neck over the cropped flow blue semi-sheer top. Taken in twos or threes, the combination clashes. But taken together, *voilà*, you have beauty. Cher used to do this. They called her tacky, but she was ahead of her time.

Both of those women would look good in anything.

It's not exclusive to them. The weird girl look is like Harajuku. In Harajuku, there are no rules: you wear what you want, what makes you feel comfortable and fresh, whether that's Lolita, Decora, or whatever. Look at this picture. Or this. Those are traditional Japanese wooden sandals with white ankle socks, a short plaid school-girl skirt, an oversize Tool tee shirt and a thick black belt, with purple streaked hair and lots and lots of bangles. The details themselves are, well, at the most, suspect. But the combination is magical.

Looks like she just put on whatever in her closet she could reach.

It's not that easy.

There are some happy accidents, no doubt. But also work, trial and error, revision.

They're all skinny and young. And I'm not sure they're beautiful. They are interesting. Fashionable, whatever that means.

How about these guys?

Who are they?

Les Sapeurs. From the Congo. Not young, not always skinny, and not white.

They're striking, for sure. I like the banana yellow suit with the herd of goats in the background. The flamingo suit with the dark blue vest against the rusted-out truck. That is indeed striking; I'll give you that.

How about this? Can you see the beauty in this?

A large man in drag. Not sure about the beauty here.

That's Leigh Bowery.

I always liked him.

He looks like a scary clown. Like a serial killer.

How about here?

That's kind of cool. I like the flowers and the sequins. Still looks frightening.

Just as there is no detail that is necessarily excluded from beauty, there is also no human face or figure that cannot be made beautiful.

That's a big leap.

All of these photos I've shown you, from Van Herpen to the Harajuku looks to *Les Sapeurs* to Leigh Bowery, all are photos of others, yes, of the other? Not much in common.

OK.

You've no desire to change or alter any of these looks, do you? Or to become the figure you're looking at?

No, I don't want to be Leigh Bowery. Or the Harajuku girls.

Fashion is the other composing itself to be seen. Fashion is the other preparing itself for an ethical relationship. And to see the other's face in its beauty, and to respect the other as other, to let the other be. . . that's close to love.

Maybe.

If fashion prepares the other to be seen, fashion also prepares the self to see. If I'm interested in how I look, if I pay attention, then what do I do before I leave the house?

No clue.

I look in the mirror. I try to see if the details of my look fit together to create a whole. The point is that I *see*. I've learned how to look. Fashion prepares one to see, prepares one to be able to see the other. Without that practice, without the cultivated ability to carefully, actively look, we simply pass each other in the night. Fashion paves the groundwork for a possible relationship between the self and the other. That's how it's ethical.

I still can't buy it. You're still building your ethics, your aesthetics, on the broken backs of children in sweatshops. It requires tremendous forgetting and a corrupt willful blindness to see fashion as ethical.

I can see I'm not going to change your mind.

Do you want to go to a party?

Now?

Paula's party?

Yeah. It said dress warm, so it might be on her roof.

Sure. Let's go.

CHAPTER 5
MARTIN MARGIELA, "THE PLAYGROUND SHOW"

God, I've had too much to drink. You think you don't want to do this? I don't want to do this. Do you know why I do not want to do this, Mr. Dunn? Do you know why I do not want to relive my salad days as a Parisian fashion model, ooh la la, a *mannequin de cabine* for the ultra-chic Maison Margiela? I can tell you in a single word. It's the word girl. I hate the word girl. It's so hard to drink with a mask, don't you know? Let's all take our masks off, shall we? And keep them off.

They were sitting around an expensive couch in a luxurious rooftop garden underneath a Japanese pergola, flanked by a softly hissing propane heater on one side and a low-slung wooden table on the other. The stars were bright in the dark sky.

What about girl power? Doesn't the word sound fierce? Grrrrrrl. Why did he say that?

I hate the word girl. Whenever I'm with the fashion people, or at least people who knew me when I was working, I know they're thinking of me as a girl. Or now, I suppose, an ex-girl, a former girl, an aged-out girl. Aged out to what, you may ask? Aged out to a woman? A person? A human being? Please. No fucking way. Just a girl who is no longer a girl, an ex-girl. And what is a girl, you may ask? Legs, hips and a collar bone. And eyes. That's it. Nothing else. Not even a mouth. Especially not a mouth. Not even a mouth with cherry red lips, the whitest of teeth and a dazzling smile. With dimples. Because mouths can talk. Eventually all mouths talk. And who wants to listen to a girl? Who the fuck wants a girl's mouth yapping all the time? Interrupting. Breaking concentration. Articulating thoughts. Expressing desires. Bitching at one thing or another. And you know what else mouths can do, don't you, Mr. Dunn? Mouths can eat. And no one wants a girl who eats. Maybe, maybe nibble. Once in a while. But not eat. Gross. Balance is key, Mr. Dunn. If food goes in, then shit must come out. Whatever enters, exits; it's the law of the body. Nothing tastes as good as skinny feels. Either going down or coming up. You understand, Mr. Dunn, what I'm trying to say. I was never on the three-finger diet myself, but I remember always being hungry. Oh, and I smoked. Girl mouths can smoke; that's the one thing girl mouths are allowed. And drink. But not drink too much, because of the calories. And drunk girls are sloppy. But never eat. Or talk. We know what else mouths can do, but let's not go there, not quite yet. Am I embarrassing you, Timo?

Not at all, although I would like another drink.

You're leaving me alone with Mr. Dunn?

I'll return. Maybe this will be useful for him.

Can you bring me another gin and ice?

Sure.

Good gin, please. Monkey 47. They have it.

Monkey 47.

Legs, hips and a collarbone, that's what girls are, Mr.

Dunn. Human hangers. Tits and ass optional—although a little of both can go a long way, too much not so much. And eyes never hurt, at least for editorial. She stood, slightly unsteadily, and took the two steps toward the couch, where she turned and sat down next to him. She smelled good, like the English countryside. Do you know why you're talking to me; do you know why we are even having this conversation? Do you know the one thing that makes me extraordinary? The one accident of nature that has given me this life, this life of being a girl, and now an ex-girl? Can you take a guess, Mr. Dunn?

I have no idea.

Can't you humor me and try? Is it my sparkling per-sonality? No, that's not that, is it? Even when I'm drunk, I don't sparkle. My intelligence? No. Talent. What is my talent, Mr. Dunn? What was I good at? What in my career was I exceptional at?

I don't know.

I told you I was a fit model, a *mannequin de cabine*. Where I stood still most of the time. Is that a talent, standing still? Does that require anything special, Jona-than? To stand still for hours? To stand still so someone else can form me into a vision he has created? So someone can fashion me to correspond to an image in his head? It requires no talent, no special skill. A blank canvas has no talent. A bolt of cloth has no talent. I don't think I was even particularly good at it, the standing still. Especial-ly when I couldn't read my books, or when Martin had to concentrate so we couldn't talk. What else did I do? I walked on a catwalk. Is walking a talent, Mr. Dunn? Is walking so that clothes someone else has made are shown at their best effect a talent? No, walking is not a talent. I had to learn that walk, and I sucked at it. That model walk—expressionless face, straight line, one foot almost crossing the other, heel first, chin up—I was terrible. At least Martin and Rei didn't require heels, like Lee did. She rotated her right foot on her ankle. I liked Lee, but I couldn't wear his shoes. Standing still and walking, not exactly a formidable skill-set.

She took another drink and rolled an ice cube in her mouth briefly, then spit it back into her glass. So if it's not my personality, not my talent, what is it? My looks, right? That's what made me a girl. How would you describe my looks, Jonathan?

Don't do this.

You've seen photos of me when I was a girl: what did you see?

He shook his head and stared at his drink.

Use your words.

I don't want to do this.

You're the writer; how would you describe what I looked like? What were my girl-looks? What was my defining feature? How'd that bitch Alexandra put it, both guttersnipe and queen? I like the word guttersnipe.

As do I.

But what about your words, Mr. Dunn? I was on billboards, for Chrissakes. Why? You've seen pictures, right? You have done your homework, you have seen my fashion photos, correct?

Of course.

What was it, then? What made the girl? You're not going to answer. Ok, I'll make it easy for you. Maybe you can't remember, maybe those images of the girl me didn't stick. That's fair. We all look alike, right? So, look at me now. She stood and pivoted to face him, with her waist about a foot away from the tip of his nose. If he leaned forward slightly, he could look down at the floor between his shoes. If he leaned back, his gaze would naturally move upwards to her breasts and neck. He was aware of other people looking at them. What do you see, Jonathan?

He focused on the sky-blue *fleur de lis* pattern between his shoes. Peripherally, he could see her turning on her left foot, pirouetting slowly. What the fuck was she doing? When she completed the turn and was facing him again, she repeated loudly, as if to ward off any suggestions of intimacy: You're the writer; what do you see?

They remained frozen in that position, Millie obdurately vertical, precisely ninety degrees with the floor, and Jonathan bent forward, his gaze anxiously averted. She stepped forward and inserted her foot between his, forcing him to lean back and raise his head to avoid her thigh. Their eyes met, and she hesitated for just a beat before retreating slightly.

You still don't know, do you? You still don't know what

made me a girl. I've no ass, no hips, no tits and no lips. My nose is too long and sometimes had to be shortened in post. I do have a neck, but depending on the angle, it can seem inadequate to support my rather large and heavy head. My hair is meh, always has been. As she spoke, she moved her finger to touch whatever body part she was describing, like a TV gameshow hostess. My cheekbones are ok, but my collarbone juts out, which became a problem when I was on drugs. Heroin chic was a thing, but Auschwitz chic was not. My skin is dark, and I have big pores. It's also on the oily side, especially on my forehead and near my eyes. My eyes are a striking green, sometimes sea green, sometimes grass green, sometimes closer to turquoise, depending on the light and what I'm wearing. She abruptly folded down on the seat beside him, swirled her drink around, then took a sip. Do you think it's my eyes, Mr. Dunn? Do you think my eyes are what got me where I am today?

You're not even looking at me. C'mon, Jonathan, look into my eyes and tell me what color you see. C'mon, humor me. What color do you see? I'm guessing, given that I'm wearing this cobalt jacket and I bronzed slightly, that they're somewhere between a hazel grass and seafoam. Am I right?

He turned and looked. Her eyes appeared surprisingly gentle, in a sort of *noblesse oblige* way, given her loutish tirade. Gentle and even, dare he say, vulnerable? I would say more seafoam than grass. More Gulf of Bothnia than

St Andrews fairway.

Oh well done Mr. Dunn. But my eyes, as striking as they may be, are not the reason I'm here, sitting on this lovely Ethimo sofa, talking to you in your black Nietzsche priest outfit. And my calling my own eyes striking should not be ascribed to conceit or pride since I did nothing to earn or deserve them: they are, first and always, simply a genetic accident, a chromosomal coincidence, a P protein luck of the draw. Anyway, you don't need seafoam or hazel grass or ice princess or brilliant midnight eyes to walk on a catwalk or model *toiles* in the *atelier flou*. Eyes may be important for editorial, and they loved these peepers at Hermès, but no one looks at eyes on the runway. You really can't see them anyway. So no, these glorious orbs of the sea's reflection bright are, alas, not what made me a girl.

She leaned back and stretched out her legs in front of her. Her silver skirt rode up briefly on her thighs, but she pulled it down quickly. No, the one part of me, the one part of my body that made me a girl, that gave me this life, that created oh so very many choices for me, the one part that perhaps determined my fate, if we believe in such a thing . . . can you guess? You'll laugh when I tell you. Can you guess? No. The one thing that made me a girl, two things really, are my tibiae. Ta da. Simple as that. Rather anticlimactic, no? Two bones below my knees are the most important thing about me. My. Two. Tibiae. Sounds like a song.

You are looking confused, Mr. Dunn. The tibiae have

everything to do with how tall we are. Not only do they lengthen the leg, they also determine overall height, toe to crown. Every girl I know has lengthy shins. Thighs may enchant, with their erotic ambivalence, sometimes soft, sometimes hard, and an extended torso delights, but it's those two workmanlike calf bones what make the girl. Jerry, Jerry Hall has exquisite tibiae, absolutely gorgeous. As did Veruschka. From the pictures I've seen.

Marlena Dietrich.

I know the photos you're thinking of. Marlena Dietrich, exactly.

And she was what, five five, five six?

It's odd, don't you think, that there's nothing one can do about one's tibiae. There are no exercises or diets to elongate the bone, no care one can really give. No nurture there, just nature. Maybe drinking your milk. I hated milk as a kid.

You can get shin splints.

Yes. Do you know what shin splints are?

It has something to do with running. I think.

She shrugged. One can, what's the word, sculpt one's calves, but calves have nothing to do with height, with a girl's identity, a girl's existence. It's also strange that as far as I can tell, tibiae don't age. They don't curve, bend, or suddenly snap. The covering skin (there's no real flesh there) can eventually sag, I suppose, but by that time other structures have already collapsed, fallen and pooled. Most of the other parts of me, in the transition from girl to no-longer, have changed, at least somewhat. But my tibiae, at least as far as I can tell, remain the same. More constant than my mind, that's for sure.

That's one of the bones people often find, isn't it, when they're looking for bodies, or in ancient gravesites?

Nothing you can do about your tibiae, not one damn thing. Pure genetics. My father was tall, but my mother was not. All the height comes from his side of the family. My sister is five ten, my brother five nine. If the goddess of sexual reproduction had plucked a different combination of genetic marbles from my two parents' bowls, I'd be a vastly different person, with an infinitely different life. Two bones, Mr. Dunn. Two bones. That's what made me a girl. And now an ex-girl.

She finished her drink and sucked her last ice cube into her mouth. She lowered her glass down to her lap and looked around. I wonder where Timo is. Now I'm not suggesting that long tibiae are all that are required: no, other attributes—small waist, nice skin, cut cheekbones, healthy hair—are certainly important and add to your overall look. But I am saying that you can have all of these; you can be what everyone in your high school calls beautiful, but if you have short tibiae, you'll be lucky to get a call-back from the Orvis outlet in western PA, if you know what I mean.

My drink is long gone. Do you mind if I smoke? We're outside. She put her glass down on the floor and brought her small red purse with an embossed T enclosed by a looping C. She rooted around and brought out her cigarettes in a dull silver case. She quickly snapped open the tin, extracted a cigarette, put it to her mouth and closed the case, returning it to her bag. She looked at him for a moment, but as he carried neither lighter nor matches, he remained motionless. A thin gold lighter appeared, held delicately by a thumb and forefinger; the large, almond-shaped nails painted to simulate a cut block of polished marble.

Millie leaned forward to the flame, lit her cigarette, exhaled, then sat back and looked up. The lighter and marble accompaniment swiftly retreated to the slim black pocket of a very young person of indeterminate gender in a black, off-the-shoulder jumpsuit, the bodice and right shoulder joined by a polished chrome triangle clasp. The shoulders and upper arms were chiseled and powerful, but the hands, wrists and throat seemed delicate and fragile. The overall effect was definitely ambivalent. Any breast definition was obscured by the folds of the musou black bodice. They (singular) were now leaning backward as if in reaction to their forward movement offering the lighter. Jonathan looked down at their shoes, as footwear was often significant, but they were completely hidden by the drape of the trousers. You're very welcome. It's sometimes hard to find fire when you need it. The voice was expressive but regular, its pitch and modulation perfectly indeterminate. Don't I know it, Millie laughed. Who are you wearing? It's lovely, but I don't recognize it.

No Sesso.

No sex, huh? That's great. I don't know them.

They're from here, New York. You should look them up.

I should. Do you mind if I touch the fabric?

Please.

What is it?

Viscose, with a touch of elastane.

Thank you.

You are most welcome.

Are we drunk enough to talk about sex? I mean am I drunk enough? That's the real story, isn't it, girls and sex? What we can do to *you* with our girl mouths. Pure generosity without need. You must have thought about sex, Mr. Dunn. Sex and fashion, like gin and tonic. We're the same age, right, more or less?

We were born on the same day.

Really? That's wild. So we are the same age. Where did you grow up?

All over. I was born in California, went to high school in Rhode Island, college in Buffalo, grad school in New York.

I'm from Colorado, as the internet has told you. You remember the 90's, yes?

The go-go nineties.

The go-go nineties indeed. Although there was AIDS. Her brow furrowed and she took a drag of her cigarette with a perfect French inhale.

She laughed suddenly, changing moods immediately, like a child. And grunge. *Oy vey!* Thank God I was in Paris. No wonder they took drugs. No wonder I took drugs. Although I do like the boots.

I like the music.

Yeah, I never have. Anyway, there was AIDS, there was grunge, but we still fucked through all that. Somehow. Although sex with a girl is never about the sex. And it's certainly not about the girl.

Really?

Really. I could tell you stories, Mr. Dunn, stories that would likely shock or titillate, but stories I'd rather not relive. She took another drag from her cigarette and looked around. Where the fuck is Timo? I started out in an OK mood, but now not so much.

Anything I can do to help? Do you want me to get you a drink?

No, Timo will be back. But there is something you can do for me. Will you answer a question for me? It's not a personal question, although it kind of is, maybe. But you need to answer honestly. If you answer my question honestly, I'll tell you one of my stories.

For the book?

Or not. We're still talking about why I hate being a girl, now ex-girl.

I'll try.

Fair enough. She performed another flawless French inhale. Can you tell me, Mr. Dunn, why men are so sexually obsessed with young girls just on this side of sexual viability? Either side, really.

I don't know.

What is it about the hairless, the barely formed, the innocent and inexperienced that seems to excite so?

I don't know.

Is it porn?

I don't know.

Because you see, Jonathan, there doesn't exist the same unquenchable obsession from our side. Women can, I admit, find younger men attractive, but that attraction almost never extends to those who can't yet drive. And the attraction women may find for younger men, notice I didn't say boys, is due almost exclusively to the physiological. Younger men are often more physically functional than their older counterparts. And while I further admit there can be some pleasure in educating the apprentice, this pleasure is not due to the corruption of the pristine, but rather, it's the pleasure most women are familiar with, that of preparing the novice, the same way we educate our sons and daughters for their anticipated lives outside the home. But that pleasure seems tied to utility rather than transgression.

Why do men want to fuck girls? I mean, it can't be that enjoyable, can it? Girls don't know what they're doing, don't know how to either respond or create with imagination or élan. Girls have little technique, barely know what goes where, so where's the fun? Is it the thrill of marking untouched snow? Of boldly going where no man has gone before, to quote a television show we're both familiar with? Is it the competition, something to tell the bros at work? Hey dude, I was her first. The pain, the blood, the fear. . . does that excite you? I just can't wrap my head around this Lolita fixation: any possible explanation I can come up with makes men seem monstrous.

Not all men want to fuck virgins.

But all men want to fuck girls. Even with older girls—and by older I mean twenty-two or twenty-three—there's the expectation that they'll at least approximate the virginal: hairless, thoughtless, speechless, shaved, wrinkle free and ready to rock. Ready to wear. Men don't want sexual partners; you want penis envelopes, something wet and tight to provide the right amount of guilt-free friction. That's what a girl is. That's what a girl does.

I don't know what to say.

Oh, I know, I sound like one of these dreary feminists, don't I? And while there are many things a girl can't be, a feminist tops the list. Just below *tomber enceinte*. Anyway, you are being honest; I can tell that you honestly don't know what to say. I will now keep my part of the bargain and narrate, with a dry throat, one of the many sexually suspect incidents that occurred to me. This is certainly not the worst thing that ever happened, not by far. But it is typical, in a strange way, par for the course. I don't see an ashtray, do you? I don't want to use my empty glass. It was a year or two before I started working for Hermès,

Her eyes have seen everything. They've seen Picasso in his studio and the cords of corpses piled high at Dachau. They've seen napalm at St. Malo and a double-breasted suit from Pidoux with a leopard fur collar and pockets. They've seen squat nuns looking for their Father Superior in the rubble of a bombed church and the image of a hand brilliantly diffracted into shards of pure light. These are the distressed eyes of Man Ray's "Glass Tears" as well as those hidden by the alien-looking ovals of the US Army gas mask. Now they're gazing up at something to the camera right. The brows are neat and arched. Her nose is too big and solid from the angle. Her lips are full, and formed into an absolutely straight line, with just the slightest deviation from the horizontal. The mouth is where all emotion and judgment stop. The mouth negates any interest or disdain the eyes might suggest.

when I was a bit strung out. I went to England to walk for Lee, Alexander McQueen, and was having a hard time getting back to Paris; I don't remember why. My agent set me up for this editorial shoot, not Chanel, *British Vogue* or Demarchelier, but not too far off, names I recognized, maybe a couple of steps down. There you are. I was beginning to fear you'd ditched us.

I had difficulty locating your Monkey. I had to go to two floors downstairs.

Thank you so much. I was just about to tell Jonathan one of my hashtag metoo adventures. This will help.

Do I know this story?

Oh yes. Anyway, we were two hours at least outside London, really in the middle of nowhere on the eastern coast, this ruined castle on a desolate hill. It was freezing, and I was wearing, well, this certain designer's clothes: think tight corsets, puffy sleeves and voluminous skirts, lots of lace and flounce. Retro, in a way, but not retro to any one particular era or style. Combo retro. Actually, rather pretty, all in all. Anyway, I was the only model working—there had been a couple of others, but they'd been let home. Just me, the stylist, the photographer and his assistant. We were doing these beauty-in-front-of-ruins kind of shots, the decay of British culture vibe, and it was getting dark. And I was cold and hungry. As I said, it

The sexuality is there, prominent but ambivalent. The woman is nude in a bathtub, small but central in the matrix of the geometric tile. Her right hand covers her neck and shoulder with a white washcloth, her right arm protects her breast. Her boots have soiled the rug directly below her face; her clothing and watch have been placed on a chair to the right, above which a small statue of a naked nymph stands on a table.

We always return to the face. Symmetrical, it sits at the exact center of the shot, and is further framed vertically by the looping shower hose above and two black boots below, and horizontally by two identical soap dishes, another large soap dish and towel bar that runs a couple of inches above the lip of the tub on the square tiled wall. Placed near the left side of the frame, to the left of the large soap dish, is a framed photographic portrait of Adolf Hitler.

was getting dark, so we moved inside to one of the few intact rooms. It was warm there; the hot lights were already set up, and I was wearing this big dress with evening gloves, so it was all good. The stylist worked on me for a bit: I drank some lukewarm tea and was hoping to wrap this up right quick. I took my place in front of the lights, and they were bright; no gel that I remember, so I couldn't see a thing. I was sitting on this bench, this pew-like thing, and he was ordering me this way and that. Then he put some music on, Queen, believe it or not. We were shooting: he was listening to The Show Must Go On and I was dreaming of fish and chips with a pint. I was listening to him and shifting around, not really concentrating, shoulder higher, pout, chin up, and then this hand reached out from behind the lights and pulled my ankle down so I'm sitting like this—she moved her hips to the edge of the couch and stretched out both legs. I was shocked, speechless. He had never touched me before. I thought maybe he was getting tired or impatient. Photographers sometimes touched you; it was not necessarily a big deal, but there was usually some warning or something: a clue that he was handsy, or that maybe you'd worked with him before, or even the way he greeted you, like with a hug and cheek kiss or something like that. Anyway, I was stunned as hell, but didn't say anything. He then told me to lean back and open my mouth. He had moved back behind the lights, and I just really wanted to get this over with, so I did what he said. Hold it right there. I held it right there. Close your eyes. I closed my eyes. Then I heard this sound, this light rhythmic pulsing. At first, I thought it was the music, but the rhythm was all off, and it was coming from the other side of where the boombox was. Pull your skirt up a little bit and open your knees, he said, and I did. He had this light, breathy voice, and his instructions were never very convincing; they always sounded more like pleas or suggestions. I began to get a little nervous, but I remember thinking that if I moved, he might want to start over, so I just lay there, still as could be, knees open, mouth open, eyes closed. The music paused and I could hear that rhythmic fluttering before Queen kicked in again.

I realized two things at once. First of all, I hadn't heard the click-whrr of the camera in quite some time and second, there was no one else in the room save the photographer and me. I had no idea where the stylist and the assistant went, but I knew they weren't anywhere near. Fuck this, I thought; if they were done then so was I. I stood up, straightened my skirt, and walked toward the door. I got past the lights and guess what I saw. You have any idea, Jonathan? Timo? I walked behind the hot lights, and it took my eyes a while to adjust, but soon enough I saw our hero, pants to his knees, dick in his hand, and what's the word the kids use, fapping away. His eyes were open. Of course they were. He gave me this little smile, complicit and cruel, that suggested that I was equally involved in his sordid activity and if I ever wanted to work again, I'd keep my mouth shut. There was also the request, in that same simpering smirk, that I should return to my position so that he could finish and we could continue the shoot. I was so disgusted and angry—and really didn't care if I ever worked again— that I just found the door and walked out into the freezing night. The stylist gave me a ride back to London. He said the photographer did that all the time and had a lot of friends in high places. He also said that there were a lot of photographers who were worse.

I got back to London and called my booker who was shocked, shocked! at such unprofessional be-

Lee Miller is bathing in Hitler's bathtub on the day of his death.

havior. Bitch set me up. Never worked with her again. I've had worse things happen to me, but that's the one that still pisses me off the most.

Why, do you think?

She took a long sip of her drink. A couple of reasons. First of all, he didn't even make a pass at me. Shoots can get sexy. Not always, but sometimes: I'm in nice clothes, I'm all made up, it's a beautiful place, I'm feeling pretty, everyone's looking at me, maybe some champagne, maybe something stronger, yeah, it can be fun, sexy. I've never fucked anybody on set, but I've gone back to a few hotel rooms, sure. This place was bleak: I was cold and cranky, true, but this douchebag never even tried. There was no vibe there, and I can't even remember what he looked like other than that sick little smirk, but if you want something, ask. Pass me a note, whisper in my ear, touch me on the elbow, make eye contact, something. I would have firmly declined, but that's the game, right, and what girl from fourteen on hasn't learned to avoid and extricate, but he didn't even give it a shot, so to speak. He just hid behind his lights and camera, whacking his noodle.

But you know what really pisses me off? You write about narcissism, Mr. Dunn, and how women who like to be photographed or looked at are often called narcissistic. I can't imagine anyone more narcissistic than this guy. Think about it: this dude got me all dolled up, arranged the lighting, the costuming, the setting, posed me just so with spread knees and opened mouth, and tried to fuck me *from ten feet away.* So I wouldn't notice and do some-thing to mess up his perfect picture. This was his vision and his vision only, and that's all he wanted to fuck. He didn't even want me; he just wanted his image made flesh, his picture in his head made three-dimensional; that's what he was trying to get off on. He was trying to fuck himself through me. Can you imagine anything more de-grading than that?

Because I think that's what men think girls are for. They're just fucking themselves. Or oth-er bros. Hey dude, I banged a model last night. That bottle service circuit is like that. That's another story. Bros just wanna be seen with beauti-ful women—it's like wearing a nice suit or

Yes, it's the very image of survival, of celebration and ablution, as we all wash off the dust of Dachau in Hitler's Mu-nich tub. It's a *mikvah* of sorts, a cleans-ing not of the feminine body, but of the body of European civilization itself. With the dirt of the boots to remind this cleansing is not total, is not permanent, but merely a moment of light in a world tending to the dark filth of death and destruction. The hope of the insouciant gaze of the bathing woman is belied by the white rug stained by the soiled boots. The eyes may look forward, but the boots will never forget.

driving a nice car. The sex is secondary, if that. God, I sound so sex negative, so Fancy Feast spinster. *No sesso.* But I'm not. I understand desire. I love desire. I under-stand what it means to lose control, to act the fool. And that never bothers me. I almost never get pissed if a man or a woman comes on to me: you have to cross all sorts of lines before I get annoyed. This is *not* an invitation, by the way, Mr. Dunn. It's not that I don't like sex, it's just that

I'm interested in at least partially mutual participation.

And you also talk about self-consciousness. Where was his self-consciousness? He didn't even care that I saw him jerking off. There's your narcissism without self-consciousness, Mr. Dunn. And let me tell you something else: girls are self-conscious from the minute they see some guy looking at them, wondering what they look like in their underwear. From the age of ten, maybe? Twelve? If anyone could use some self-consciousness, it's you.

Maybe it's all instinct.

Not you personally. I mean men in general. Most men.

I read somewhere that attraction is based on the unconscious desire for reproduction.

But girls aren't fertile. We, they, don't have the hips. We don't eat enough food to get our periods. Our boobs are primarily decorative, not functional. They function by allowing a nice drape on a Bardot blouse, but they usually can't provide the required nutrition for a growing infant. We're certainly not muscular, nor are we soft, rounded and nurturing. We're all angles, sharp elbows and cheekbones, stiletto heels and stiletto glances. We may have height, but it's a height not of accomplishment and enlightenment but of privilege and accident. The things we hunt and gather are abstract, money and power. We're no mothers in waiting; we're the opposite, the promise of immutable immortality. You can cut yourself on us, impale yourself. But you can't penetrate us. Not really.

Ah, Jesus, I'm coming off as a sexless scold, immune to

the longing caress, indifferent to the tender brush of silk on skin. And where do I get off talking about motherhood, right, with my eggs unused, having fled the barn. Or maybe I'm just missing my girlhood: the fame, fortune and pleasure of being looked at and looked after, of having a place in the world, of being wanted by others, plural. No, it's not that; it's not nostalgia. I hated being a girl. I hated being looked at and never seen, superficially celebrated for my accidental genetics.

She narrowed her eyes and looked first at Timo, then at Jonathan.

It almost seems like you're that photographer, Mr. Dunn, arranging me just so.

What? What do you mean?

Forget it.

Chapter 6
Martin Margiela, "The Flat Show"

This is a nice place. Thank you for inviting me.

After last night, I'm surprised you're here. Did Timo finally change your mind?

Believe it or not, you did.

This is another side of modeling I thought you should see, Mr. Dunn. You should grab a plate before we go. The *cacio e pepe* is very good.

I'll try it, although I did eat earlier. This is all a bit late for me.

She chuckled. My nocturnal habits are one thing I haven't aged out of. I can't eat dinner before ten.

That's when I go to bed.

The words that initially came to him to describe his situation—he was surrounded by beautiful young women—were sorely disappointing in their banality and inadequacy. He didn't have the vocabulary, perhaps there was no vocabulary, to describe the seductive charm of these creatures. It was almost as if he had entered another dimension, one of extreme loveliness and grace, or had landed on another planet, a planet where both gravity and genetics were of a different order. How could they fit all the interior organs into that wasp waist? How could those thin but shapely legs support those hips and torsos? This imaginary, fantastic world required a new language, a language that would be capable of approximating such aesthetic pleasure. Was aesthetic the right word? The fatigue and vague annoyance he'd felt on the subway ride and the walk to the restaurant (it *was* late for him) had completely disappeared, replaced by a vitality that was indifferently and impersonally sexual. It was as if he were back in his twenties. The eroticism was imaginary, imaginative, but no less real for all that.

The women here were of a different species altogether. They moved with indescribable grace and elegance. It was odd, he thought, that the word grace signified both how one moved physically in the world and God's favor toward the unworthy. Hail Mary full of grace. There was something spiritual in the way that woman brought a forkful of pasta to her lips, that one swept her hair back in a mirror, that one sat and crossed her legs. There was a magic here, an enchantment he was unused to.

The word perfection came to mind, but he immediately dismissed it. Perfection implied the realization of an ideal, and these women were not manifestations of anything other: they were simply, absolutely, utterly themselves. There was no external Platonic form they were approaching or actualizing. Which is perhaps why the word model was problematic. They weren't the perfect specimens of some imagined archetype, paradigm, or concept; they were incomparable to each other. This was not to say that the multiplication and sheer variety of lovely features and gestures played no role in the charm of the individual but that any judgment or comparison of one woman to another was impossible. Maybe. He chuckled.

I need to introduce you to Diana, our host for the evening, although I don't see her around. She was ambivalent about inviting you, Mr. Dunn. This is not really a situation for spectators here, at least those who don't pay. You'll be privy to a unique experience, one that few enjoy.

Thank you for arranging this.

You're welcome. I see you dressed up, not all black. Is that your Armani shirt?

I hope you approve.

It's not me you have to please, it's Be-Bop, Diana's assistant. Or the doorman at the Marquee.

He did, on some level, always understand that this magic was illusory: the appearance of this beauty was worked and practiced, as artificial as a Hollywood film. But this in no way detracted from his enjoyment. Perhaps it was the pandemic and quarantine. Perhaps this was the tawdry fascination of a hermit or celibate, seeing in the cheapest of bangles and gaudiest of eyeshadow the allure of goddesses and queens. He watched a woman with dark, midnight hair take the smallest sip of wine. There was nothing self-conscious in the gesture, as any self-consciousness was overcome by what, for lack of a better term, he thought of as confidence. Absolute confidence. She was used to being looked at, yes, and was indifferent to all that. Or to be more precise, there was both indifference and pleasure in that gesture: she enjoyed being looked at as much as he enjoyed looking. That wasn't it either.

He took some pasta on his plate and sat next to Millie.

I was quite drunk last night, Mr. Dunn. You'll please excuse my lack of discretion. I hope I didn't make you too uncomfortable.

No, not at all. I found it interesting. Um, is it just me, or are all these women young? They look younger than my students.

Some of these women probably *are* your students.

That could get awkward.

They're fashion models, not escorts or sex workers.

I'm not judging anybody. And speaking of writing, when can we meet to go over the photographs? Aren't you leaving on Saturday?

We can meet the day after tomorrow. And yes, I am leaving for Paris on Saturday. And yes, I need a cigarette.

The pasta is very good.

Try the *cantuccini*. And drink some wine, but pace yourself. She chuckled. We've a long night. Although you could leave at any time, I suppose.

He looked at Millie and wondered if she knew how she looked compared to the bright young things surrounding. While her face had not lost its luster nor her body its posture, they now showed the presence of an additional layer, the layer of time, evidence of experience, of knowledge earned rather than existence enjoyed. There was the slightest weariness to her, a small sadness that came not from the awareness that many of her possibilities would never be realized, but from the understanding that perhaps too many already had. He found himself wondering at what age, at what moment the balance tipped, at what moment memory overcame hope. But maybe he was projecting.

Millie.

Diana. I was looking for you. This is Mr. Dunn, Jonathan. Mr. Dunn, this is Diana. This is all her show.

You're the writer.

Yes. Thank you for inviting me.

This is all her idea. She motioned with her chin to Millie. She spent a favor on you. And it's Diana with an a. Don't forget the a.

I won't forget the a.

She turned to Millie. We're just about ready to go. You'll ride with a couple of the girls. Normally, you could ride with me, and we could talk over old times, but Be-Bop called in sick, and I got a couple of rookie civilians, so I'll need to go with them to lend moral support. I'll hit you up later. Rides will be here in five. She turned to address the room.

Rides will be here in five, ladies. She didn't have the biggest voice, but all the women put their glasses down, gathered their phones and purses, straightened their skirts, and adjusted their overshirts or shawls. Conversation ended. Let's go over the rules one more time, shall we? Rule number one—you arrive with me you leave with me. I will drop you off where I picked you up. You want to make other arrangements you do so after I drop you off.

I ain't your mama, but I am not a pimp. Rule number two no drugs. None. And watch your drinking. No one likes a lush. Rule number three no masks. I don't care if your vax record is fugazi, no covering that pretty mouth. Got it? If I, or one of my associates, catch you breaking these rules, we won't cause a scene. I will just text your name and photo to every promoter I know. I might include even include some bouncers and the like. You do not want to get on my shit list. OK. Have fun tonight. A few now opened compacts and fiddled with makeup, while others scrolled, their faces garishly illuminated by the phone screens.

This was a favor she owed, he asked.

Millie gulped the last of her wine. So, the biography begins? Let's go outside: I want to smoke.

Maybe you should get one of those vape things.

No thank you. She stood. She walked quickly out. A few feet down from the door, she turned abruptly and quickly lit a cigarette. She exhaled, leaned back against the wall and gazed past him to the curb where some of the women waited for transport.

She spoke quickly, her sentences running into one another. God, I remember this scene. Diana wasn't in charge back then, and what was his name, Fonte something, would take us all for sushi down by Fulton Market. It smelled like salmon and Chanel, always Chanel, sometimes with that faint chemical smell of poppers. She shook her head. I was a mess. She took a drag of her cigarette and looked straight at him. Martin helped secure the Hermès gig for me because he was worried about how I'd live. I'd started taking drugs when I was twenty-eight and had fallen into some disrepair. I had to quit Hermès because I looked like shit, and was really down, washed up at thirty, no education, looks going going gone, but with enough money to buy enough drugs to kill myself many times over. I came to New York to get away from all my heroin friends in Paris. Diana was a model, beautiful, yes, gorgeous, but not tall enough, who was learning the promotion side of things. She was trying to get her own agency up and going. Millie looked away and smiled. She was nice to me, kind, found me a place to stay, and tried to clean me up. When I felt better, when my skin cleared and I'd gained a little weight, I would go to her parties, the former face of Hermès, and to the clubs, Bungalow, The Roxy, even the Marquee. I don't know why I am telling you all this, Mr. Dunn. I get little pleasure from recounting my life, either to myself or to others.

These were the favors you earned, going to parties and nightclubs?

You were right to say that these are young women, Mr. Dunn, eighteen, nineteen, maybe twenty-one or two. This is an opportunity for young women to have fun, make friends, get into clubs for free, get a taste of the modeling life. It's like summer camp. For me at thirty, it was a chore. I did not dance back then, did not like to drink very much—yes, things have changed—and I was fiercely uninterested in the men I'd meet. On top of that, I was trying to stay off drugs, which is not easy to do in New York City nightclubs. I am a terrible actor, so you can imagine how irritable I appeared, every interminable night, tetchy, twitchy, and bored. The former face of Hermès could do nothing but frown. Diana saw how much I hated it and stopped asking me to participate. But I insisted. She thought she was exploiting me: I thought I was earning my keep. That's the so-called favor that is allowing you to tag along tonight.

I see.

I did that for about two years. Then went back to Paris.

What did you do after that?

Took care of my sister. Our agreement is for the narration of my life as a fashion model, is it not?

I suppose it is.

That's where it ends.

A large black SUV pulled up in front of them. A well-dressed man exited the passenger side, opened the back door, and nodded ever so slightly. Millie flicked her cigarette to the sidewalk. He followed her in. This was exciting. It had been a while since he had gone out in the city at night. Hell, it had been a while since he had gone out, period. A few nights a month to a restaurant with the fam, once or twice on a date night with Sally, and then the pandemic shut the whole thing down. Going out was walking down the street to pick up the takeout from Two Boots or Mamacita's.

The three women sitting across were simply gorgeous.

Two were looking at their phones and the third was looking at her phone while deftly applying or retouching eye
makeup. Hip-hop softly played in the background and a
sweet but subtle perfume filled the air. When he spoke
with his students in class or in his office, who were the
same age as the women here, he was in control: it was his
world and his game where he had many years of experience and played well. Here, he was lost. They were sitting
knee to knee, and the physical proximity was disconcert-
ing—no dais, no chairs, and no desk—and his students
at school didn't wear body glitter, micro-minis, or four-
inch heels to talk to him about Bernd and Hilla Becher.
He didn't want to be caught ogling, so he stared out the
window and snuck glances in the reflection. He turned
to face Millie, but she seemed irritated and bored, and
he took her earlier story as a warning. He didn't want to
analyze the individual details of his companions, as he
had done with the photographs of Millie, but rather just
enjoy the generalized feeling of a heightened vitality that
was almost painful. He turned back to the window and
looked out at the streets. He felt expansive, in tune with
the night.

The limo jerked to an abrupt stop, and a tube of red
lipstick flew out of one of the girl's hands and landed in
his lap. He and the woman looked down at the bright red
cylinder that rested obscenely on the crotch of his brand-
new jeans. Time stood still. My God. After some interminable interval, he snatched the tube from his groin and

held it gingerly to the girl, who took it calmly and, with a quick twist, retracted the stick into its case and placed it into the tiny metallic purse she wore on her wrist. He considered jumping from the now moving car but understood that would be even more pathetic. He no longer felt invisible.

Damn, dude. Your face redder than the lipstick.

The woman directly facing him giggled, leaned forward, and lightly touched his knee with her fingertips, for which he was, and would be, eternally grateful. You are like three shades redder, fire engine or tomato.

Was that Dior?

Yes it was. My color, Lucky. He was like Lady Red or Redvolution.

Dior's expensive.

I did a shoot for Nordstrom. Got a whole box, all different shades.

I like the paint. My guy does a great job. Good old Maybelline.

You have a guy do yours?

Not all the time. He's my neighbor. He says when I get famous to take him along.

I wish I had a guy. I hate doing my face.

I hate these fucking heels.

I'd wear heels every day if I had someone do my face.

You have such a pretty face. Probably don't even need much. A little concealer, some lipstick and you're good to go.

Uh uh. My skin oily like olives.

You ever hear of rice powder?

Rice powder? Don't that make you white AF?

You can get it in different shades. Takes away the shiny. My guy swears by it.

I did a Japanese shoot once. For whisky. I was like a geisha, you know, with that white face and red and black around the eyes. They use this thick paste, like clown make-up. Oshiroi, it's called. It's made of rice.

Did you go to Japan?

If only. Queens. Astoria to be precise.

Why is there so much traffic tonight? I'm thirsty.

Uh huh.

Not thirsty thirsty. Just thirsty. I want to get my drink on.

I hear that. I'm in a Cristal mood for sure.

Please drink me up/ Champagne Rosé.

It's my game/Please fill my cup/Champagne Rosé One bottle, two bottles, three bottles, four bottles, five bottles.

Love that jam.

How many times you done this?

Clubbing? Six months. Since I started school. I've seen you before.

I've seen you before too. Not you though.

This is just my third time.

Did you go to the Hamptons?

Yeah, that was a trip. We had what, six of us in that little cabin?

Yeah, and no AC.

The limo stopped and the driver exited quickly, opened the door on his side and waited. He followed the three women out of the car, Millie trailing. They stood on the street near the curb and gathered themselves. He counted eight women texting or adjusting their makeup and clothes. The limo zoomed away. A crowd of twenty to thirty milled about on the sidewalk, their backs to the street. Millie lit a cigarette and started talking to one of the women they had ridden with.

Another car drove up and stopped, disgorging Diana, an extremely young-looking man (boy really, and very handsome) and two other women. As if choreographed, two large men in black tank tops and shaved heads appeared and began to clear a path through the crowd toward the now visible entrance. He thought briefly of the stories of Studio 54. Diana's young man quickly followed as Diana guided the women into a single file line behind him. He followed the women, Millie following him. The crowd resisted ever so slightly. They weren't angry—after all, why get upset at the arrival of attractive young women joining a party you'd likely (maybe) attend? —merely annoyed at having their physical boundaries violated. There was perhaps the slightest resentment at the outward manifestation of class difference, similar to when one watches business-class passengers board airplanes. But again, these women were beautiful, and they were there to enhance everyone's enjoyment of the night. He was what was wrong with this picture, an aging, broke-looking killjoy, an egg-head, a fucking academic of all things. Someone's dad. If anyone saw him at all. He wished he'd worn something else. But what? He couldn't dress like he had money. The best he could do would be to appear like some aging artist, a photographer, someone who knew the scene but whose gaze was disinterested and professional. Maybe that was the role to adopt.

The crowd moved reluctantly, begrudgingly, and almost all were facing the entrance, so the going was slow.[10]

---

10 Is there such a thing as a fascist photograph, a photograph that is essentially fascist? There are, obviously, Nazi photographers and Nazi photographs. Part of that determination has to do with the omnipresence of Nazi imagery. Almost everyone in the West can recognize Nazi symbology, and the imagery from Riefenstahl to Buchenwald, from the anonymous snapshots of the SS at *Kehlsteinhaus* to the formal portraits of Hitler and Eva Braun, is familiar and immediately identifiable. These are Nazi photographs. These are photographs of Nazis (or their terrible work).

Is fascism and photography a different story? If there is a difference, can it be traced merely to the ubiquity of the visual tropes? In other words, is the difference between Nazi photography and fascist photography traceable to the fact that while everyone knows who Hitler and Goering were and what they looked like, Mussolini and his fascist compatriots don't have the "brand recognition" of their German allies? Other than *Il Duce*, can you readily picture an Italian fascist in your head? Is it the horror factor, the fact the German and Austrian Nazi's were the perpetrators of the Final Solution, while Italian Fascists had no such murderous project? Is it some combination of the two, fame and horror?

What do we see when we look at portrait photographs of people whose identity we don't know? We look for more information. We look at the context outside the frame. Are these school photos, found in a drawer? Mug shots, ID prints, publicity stills? Wedding portraits, semi-professional or professional? Are they fine art prints hung in a gallery? A museum? What language accompanies? Captions, titles? Other explanations or elucidations? Are the photos illustrative, surrounded by text? Or mounted with care and careful illumination on a white wall? Is there a single image, a connected series, or multiple but various figures?

And what of the information inside the frame? The costumes and clothing? Are there props? What kind? What are the hairstyles? The makeup? And the setting? Is it indoor? Outdoor? Is it realistic or artificial? Is the setting historical, that is recognizably tied to a specific time and place? Or is it generalized and vague, or even specific but unknown? And then there are the technical questions of print size, media, post-production, format etc.

And what does all this have to do with fascism?

We will start with a context, with the name Ghitta Carell. There are portrait photographers who are more famous, more important than their subjects: Man Ray, certainly, Richard Avedon, Cecil Beaton at times. There are other photographers whose reputations just about equal those of the people whom they photograph: Irving Penn, Annie Lebowitz, Peter Lindbergh perhaps. And there are still other photographers who drift just on this side of anonymity. These are photographers whose names do little to connote a style, a preoccupation or a readily discernible effect: their names signify a grouping of images but little else. And then, finally, there are the anonymous photographers, the unnamed (or barely named) documentary witnesses to the fame of others. Ghitta Carell fits into the third group.

The name will first be a function of selection. Under the name Ghitta Carell, we choose ten or so similar looking photographs. We chose a random image, say figure 1 (for purposes of this essay, I will initially refer to the reproductions without any title, caption or other distinguishing referent, simply as "figure 1," "figure 2" etc.). It's a classic black and white portrait of a woman, three quarter length, hands defiantly on hips and eyes defiantly staring into the camera. A thick reflective belt bisects the double-breasted tunic dress. The face is strong, masculine, and topped with a soft alpine hat with a jaunty feather. It's a studio shot, the background a simple white wall, the figure's shadow prominent. Although there is no overt or precise time reference, the photograph is nevertheless dated by the style of the picture: the black and white, the soft focus and hard gaze of the face suggest a pre-50's era, somewhere between 1930 and 1945. There's nothing terribly remarkable or memorable about the portrait other than the fact that the face seems vaguely familiar. She seems wealthy, confident and well dressed. There is something self-important about the image, but whether that stems from the figure, its context (i.e. its placement in this essay) or some combination, that's hard to say. If we add a bit more information, we see that the photograph is dated 1938. The woman and the photograph both appear to be European, so 1938 would place it at the beginning of the Second World War. The woman's gaze starts to come into focus just a bit, as her facial expression carries the undeniable indication of power. What I termed defiance earlier is not the rebellion of a resistance movement or underdog army: it belongs to (is) the threat, not the threatened. We add a name to the photograph, Edda Ciano.

Initially, the name adds less information than the year. For many, the name Edda Ciano has little significance. The name is Italian, and in the year in 1938 we think of fascism, certainly, but there's not much to suggest any overt political context. Is there?

A quick Google search indicates that Ciano is a married name and that the subject's birth was *Mussolini*. Edda Mussolini. Ah-ha. The meanings become clearer now, better defined and pointed. Edda Mussolini, the daughter of *Il Duce*, Benito Mussolini, would have been a powerful, formidable figure in 1938, important and confident. The details begin to fall into place: the Futuristic metallic belt and the Tyrolean hat become historically and symbolically significant. The face acquires a definitive reference as well. The vague feeling we had before of familiarity becomes defined—the jawline, as well as the eyes of the woman, can be traced to the image, no matter how nebulous, we have of her father. We see the same strength of will, the same hardheadness, the same self-assurance.

It is not a stretch to see Carell as the unofficial court photographer of fascist Italy. In addition to her photographs of Edda Mussolini, her client list included Edda's infamous father, as well as many members of the House of Savoy—the ruling family of Italy at the time—the family of the poet Filippo Tommaso Marinetti, and the family from the Houses of Pavoncelli, Patrizi and Delfino, all royally fascist. (There are also photos of Cardinal Francis Spellman and Walt Disney, which suggests Carell didn't limit her fascists to European nobility). It is important to note that not all Savoy royalty unambivalently succumbed to the fascist *dictat*. The Principessa Mafelda Savoy (figures 2 and 3), for example, was imprisoned at Buchenwald and died there. Maria Jose di Savoy (figure 4) tried to arrange a separate peace between Italy and the United States in 1943. Even Edda eventually broke with her father. In 1943, Edda's husband, the Count di Ciano, denounced Benito and was set to be executed. Edda tried to blackmail Hitler in an attempt to save her husband's life. Her father ignored his daughter's pleas and had his son-in-law killed, after which the strong Futurist woman of Carell's portraits disguised herself as an Italian peasant and escaped to Switzerland. Carell herself is of Jewish origin.

Millie kept smoking behind him. From what he could tell, the crowd was composed of separate clumps of men and women, three or four to a unit, the men in collared shirts and jeans, the women in ostensibly sexy dresses and heels or wide flowing pants and halter tops and heels. Some looked anxious. A few were wearing masks. The women were not as poised as those with whom he had arrived; poised was the best word somehow. The crowd looked heterosexual and mostly white. After a few moments of their slow parade, they made it to the entrance. He quickly found himself inside the doorway, where he could now hear the heavy thump thump thump of the dance music. He felt the bass in his stomach, and he felt a surge of adrenaline pump through his blood. He was handed a thin white paper wristband, which, with some trouble, he attached.

Unimpeded, they quickly moved through an elegant hallway and through a couple of doors and finally into the club proper. The space was large for New York, with booths and small tables arranged in front of the raised DJ booth. This ain't no Mudd Club. He remembered a black beauty night seeing Sonic Youth at CBGB and fingerbanging the drummer from L7, c'mon c'mon c'mon c'mon. Flashing lights and fog machines accompanied the loud electronic music. The floor was about half full of people dancing and drinking, some with glow sticks, some with N95 masks. It had been probably a decade at least since he'd been to a nightclub, maybe just after Addie was born.

And dance clubs were never his thing anyway. He was always more of a Knitting Factory/Downtown Beirut/Luna Lounge guy. He liked drinking more than dancing. But still, this was more than OK.

He began to follow the line of women as it snaked around the wall and made for a couple of empty booths and tables near the center of the floor. He felt Millie tugging on his sleeve.

We're upstairs.

What? I can't hear you.

We're upstairs. Those tables aren't for us. She pointed to a mezzanine behind them. UPSTAIRS! she repeated.

He followed as she u-turned from the line and purposefully strode back to the stairs behind. Both men and women watched her. He wondered if people thought they were a couple, and that possibility pleased more than he would have liked. She moved well, the dim light hiding some of her age tells.

The stairs were wide enough so he could walk beside rather than behind her. They were stopped at the top of the stairs by a bored looking woman with a silver Warhol wig and matching dress. After a mimed exchange, she escorted them to a small table near the railing overlooking the dance floor. The balcony was somewhat less crowded, but they were still quickly surrounded by young bodies twisting and turning every which way. He sat down on a couch indicated by the hostess. He quickly checked his iphone for the time. It was ten minutes to one.

So this was the scene. He wondered what Millie wanted him to see. He found Diana's group milling about two tables and couches near the DJ booth. A few men had infiltrated the circle, and he noticed women in skimpy blue outfits arranging ice buckets and glasses on the tables. He could use a drink himself. Three lithe bodies (he'd need to find a new, less cliché vocabulary) cavorted frantically on his left, their bodies twisting violently in space. In a corner, where the railing met the wall, a couple (one of the few couples he'd seen) single-mindedly entwined themselves. Laser lights flickered and smoke filled the air. A woman in a very short skirt bumped their table hard with her left thigh. The music played, loud and relentless. He felt edgy in ways he hadn't felt in a long time. This was good.

Speaking of that drink. He guessed drinks were at least twenty bucks a pop: he had a hundred in cash plus his credit cards. He would have to buy Millie's drinks for sure. He spotted a crowded bar downstairs to his right, but short of leaping over the railing and plunging fifteen or so feet down; he wasn't sure how to get there. There was likely a bar somewhere upstairs, but he didn't want to stand up and look around like he was some bridge and tunnel dude from Bay Shore.

He leaned over to Millie and mimed raising a glass to his mouth. I could use a drink, he added uselessly.

She nodded.

He exaggerated a searching for something face. Where's the bar?

She shrugged and stood up. Her height still surprised him. As he was looking up at her, he noticed a young woman in what looked like a short blue leather jump suit and a white cowboy hat maneuver through the crowd toward their table carrying a loaded tray. She arrived, conferred with Millie, then sat an ice bucket, a bottle of Patron and two rocks glasses down on the table. Their prayers were answered. He wondered how much this would cost. The woman removed a small bowl with lime slices from the ice bucket, filled the glasses with ice, uncorked the bottle and poured two glasses. Smiling at him, she skipped away. Millie sat down and took her glass, clinked his and took a long sip. Cheers. He took a drink from his glass.

I used to drink tequila, back in the day, she said. Now it's usually gin. Drink clear never fear, an old model's tale.

I can't hear you.

She frowned and shook her head, then leaned toward him and almost yelled, Diana sent the bottle. She remembered I like tequila.

He gave her the thumbs up. She nodded, then turned away. Free booze. And not even his birthday. Their birthday.

Three identical blonde women took selfies next to him, their backs to the dance floor. A thin young body in a full-length rabbit suit slumped in a chair on his left and began to paw the thigh of a woman adjacent.

The music slowed a bit but somehow seemed to get louder. He heard an Arabic voice in the background, a drone underneath that, and thick deliberate dance beats under that. Many of the dancers turned toward the DJ booth and pumped their fists (and perhaps cheered, he couldn't be sure). Two women to the left threw their hands in the air and, snapping their fingers, began to belly dance to the Arabic rhythm, which was getting more and more prominent. A very high pitched and very girlish voice started singing breathily in French, and Millie shot up, almost knocking her drink over. She held her hands over her head and moved her hips. She danced with a stiffness that cheered him. He noticed the percussion take the lead, and the dancing surrounding became slightly more frenetic. He took a long drink from his tequila (he would have to slow down). The Arabic voice returned to prominence. Millie turned to him, clapping her hands in rhythm. She bent down and leaned over to speak loudly into his ear. He caught the slightest whiff of cigarettes and tequila. I love Jane Birkin. I saw this concert; I was there. At the Odéon. That smile. He could barely hear her and didn't know who Jane Birkin was. Jane was so beautiful.

The breathy French voice returned as Millie returned to her dancing. He squeezed a lime slice into what was left of his drink and filled it again halfway. He looked down and noticed a small conga line of women holding brightly lit fireworks proceed from the downstairs bar toward the middle of the dance floor, where they stopped at a table and began to dance. A group of men clustered around the women, reminding him of insects attracted to light. He soon understood, from the way the fireworks were handled and manipulated, that they were attached to bottles of some kind and that he was, in fact, witnessing the rather silly attempt to make the mundane action of drink service into something spectacular. That was. . . something. He wondered why they didn't get a sparkler with their tequila.

A serious low beat began to gather volume underneath the Arabic chanting and the fragile French singing. The music was changing, now darker with synthesizers and sequencers, the tempo faster, the melody more jagged and mechanical. Millie's hips kept time with the now faded Arabic rhythm for a while, but eventually succumbed to the conquering electronic bass and glitchy synthesized melody. Hips stopped, she stood still for a few moments, then sat down almost heavily. *Je m'appelle Jane et je t'emmerde,* she sang to herself.

He could see through the smoke and the laser lights that the fireworks were extinguished (or had burned out) and the bottles placed on two tables near the center of the floor. Men, with a few interspersed women, sat or milled about while others danced around. He looked for Diana or one of the women he had ridden in with again and eventually saw the brunette who was sitting across from Millie bouncing up and down in a group by the stage. He found the other two women from the limo sitting at their table, talking with two or three men who were standing about. He took a very small sip from his drink and looked at Millie, who sat straight, her back turned ever so slightly toward him.

Now what? He wondered what drugs were for sale and how to buy them. Not that he would. He guessed Millie would disapprove, and for some reason, that was enough to make that particular thought-train hypothetical. But not necessarily.

Millie turned toward him, touched his shoulder and pointed. You should watch our group, Mr. Dunn. It might give you some insight.

All he could hear was group, Dunn and insight. I can't hear you.

She leaned and spoke loudly into his ear. You should watch the women we came with, Mr. Dunn. It might be helpful.

He nodded and leaned forward. Diana was sitting at a table amongst a group of young women, her young man at her right. An amorphous cluster circled about, some dancing, some standing and drinking. He could see very few people dancing in couples. He really couldn't discern any pattern, any rhyme or reason to the dance floor crowd. The music blared, the laser lights zipped back and forth, the machine smoke hung thick, and the mass of people moved in rhythm, but he wasn't sure what else he was seeing, or was supposed to be seeing. His energy was starting to flag as the monotony of the dance music wearied, and the heavenly creatures he had ridden with had been replaced by more mundane, earthly inhabitants.

He wondered what Millie was thinking. He guessed she wasn't having the best of times and wondered why she had decided to go out and had decided to invite him.

Ever so slightly, ever so slowly, he could almost begin to distinguish a form emerging from the nebulous mass of people dancing below. The two tables occupied by Diana and her party seemed to form an irregular nucleus around which various groupings of revelers orbited. Other women assembled around other tables, but they didn't possess the gravity of Diana and her ethereal companions. He looked more closely. There did seem to be a visible centripetal influence on some of the surrounding figures. He needed to investigate more closely. He could go down and say thank you to Diana. He could see then what was really going on down in the trenches, and it would be a chance to hang out for just a bit with at least a few of the beautiful (inadequate word) women. He could hit the bathroom afterward, then rejoin Millie for a while, then perhaps bid his farewells. He wasn't seeing what he was supposed to be seeing from here: the change in point of view from 3rd balcony omniscient to 1st dancefloor person would certainly help.

He tapped Millie on the shoulder and pointed down to the dancefloor below.

I'm going to say thank you to Diana. Millie did not look pleased.

What?

He leaned closer, cupped his mouth with his hand and

shouted, I'm going to thank Diana for this bottle.

Millie shook her head and said, I think you should wait, but he was already getting up. He refilled his glass to about three-quarters and surveyed the balcony. There was a slight opening between the rabbit suit and two men in slim European-looking suits. The kissing couple in the corner had disappeared, replaced by two girls who looked like they were twelve with long colt legs, thin sharp arms, school uniform skirts and pigtails. That must be a thing, he thought. He had some difficulty making it to the stairs through the smell of sweat, dope, magic marker, and the physical impediments of indifferent drinkers and dancers. The music turned fast and unfriendly, and he could feel his edge begin to turn. When he finally did reach the top of the stairs, the woman in the silver wig and dress shone a flashlight on the staircase to help with his Orphic descent.

As he reached the floor, white and gold confetti began to fall from the ceiling. The crowd threw their hands in the air and cheered. The music changed into a fast hip-hop number with a call and response, and everyone around enthusiastically took up the response, but it was all too loud and too fast for him to make out the words. The floor was much more crowded than it appeared from above, and no one paid him the least bit of attention as he excused his way past the two sloppy drunk women in American flag sunglasses, a group of men drinking champagne from bottles and videoing each other with their phones, four or five women in bras and panties with Playboy bunny ears, etc., etc. He stumbled a bit and sloshed his drink on one of the bunny's bare shoulders, but she didn't seem to notice. He was an artist, he was Robert Heinecken, he was Man Ray, he was E.J. Bellocq.[11] It was so loud he couldn't think,

11 Initially, there is no originality or complexity evident or implied that might elevate these photographs from the documentary to the level of fine art. Like most anonymous court portrait painters or portrait photographers throughout history, Carell's work is designed to indoctrinate and flatter. With few exceptions, they are all studio portraits, and no setting or background can fix the personage in any specific place or time. There is never any information to ground the photograph in any external context. The costuming, props and hair styles *may* suggest a specific time and culture, but both the time and culture are strangely self-contained: the references—wealth, luxury, health, charity—are so universal as to be almost meaningless. In an early series of Benito Mussolini, for example (figure 2, 1933) he eschews his military tunic and wears a soft tailored sport jacket and white shirt and tie: excepting for the familiar face, he could be any affluent businessman of the time. In a later series (figure 5, 1938), he wears his military garb. Many of the other portraits follow the same composition. In figure 6, for example, we see a jaunty looking young woman in a white blouse and possibly beige pants, tightly gripping a riding crop in her left hand. Although there are intimations of wealth and status, there is absolutely nothing to tie her to a particular age or culture. Without the identifying caption (La Contessa Arrivabene 1934), the image is almost absolutely ahistorical (within certain parameters, of course). She is blonde and seemingly tall, with an overbite and bright teeth. She could certainly be German and perhaps even American. The only remarkable detail in the photo is that her blonde hair has been retouched to shine and sparkle. Postproduction enhancement is a common technique of Carell, and undoubtedly used to flatter.

Compare Carell's photos with almost any example of photos taken of German Nazi subjects during the same time. There are studio portraits of Adolf Hitler, certainly, but after he was appointed chancellor in 1933, he almost never appeared in a studio without his uniform or some other ostentatious signifier of the Nazi power, such as an armband with swastika. Furthermore, the studio is not the Nazis preferred milieu, as they much preferred external, *in suti* shots, such as figures 7 and 8 indicate. If anything, Nazi photography was defined by its iconography and

and everyone was too close, and they were moving too fast. This had been a mistake to come down to the dance floor. It had been a mistake to come at all.

He'd find Diana, and maybe the woman whose lipstick landed in his lap—he wished he knew her name—thank the both of them, maybe have a drink and then make it back up the stairs, where he'd say goodbye to Millie. But first he needed to find Diana. That was the key.

It took him some effort, but he was making progress. He soon reached a boundary of sorts, the corner of a booth and its table. He caught a glimpse of Diana and the young man through the bobbing crowd three tables away. And there was the young woman standing near, drinking champagne and talking to a couple of men. He waved and began to squeeze between the table and two men drinking shots, but suddenly felt a strong grip on his shoulder. He turned, or rather was turned, by a large man with a large scowl on his face. The man pointed back to where he had come from with his thumb. He pointed to his wristband, but the man shook his head and yelled something and pointed up to the balcony. He stepped back and the man relaxed his grip and shrugged. He got it: this was a restricted area. Maybe Diana could let him

---

its insistence on its documentary quality, on the immediate relationship between the photograph and external, recognizable reality. The Nazi's were never shy of photographing even their most atrocious acts, as the archive is full of images similar to figures 9 and 10, where both Nazi iconography and unambiguous acts of murder are foregrounded and conspicuous.

in. He waved again, but although she was looking in his direction, she didn't see him. The young woman was still drinking champagne.

He looked at the men accompanying. They weren't wearing suit jackets, but they did look polished and prosperous, although he noticed a slight turkey neck beneath the open collar of one of the men. He gave a little wave but she didn't see. He spotted another of the models from the limo, the one with thick red hair, sitting and laughing with a man with a shaved head. He didn't feel comfortable enough to wave, so he just watched. The man laughed, then tried to rise, and stumbled slightly. Was he hammered? The man steadied himself and made it to his feet, then walked stiffly away. A few feet away, another man sat at a table talking to another one of the women. His right ear was enormous. He took another drink of his now watery tequila and looked around. Covetous smiles, severe gestures, quick laughter, the odd wrinkle, a slight paunch, laugh lines, raptor eyes. . . all of the men were well coifed, expensively dressed, fit and affluent. And they were all at least thirty years older than the women they were with.

He eventually made it back to Millie. He sat heavily.

I see you're back, she said.

I wasn't welcome down there, he said.

No, she said, probably not. She smiled, not unkindly. She poured water from a pitcher into his tequila glass. Here, drink some water.

He gulped it down.

Books are of no use down there, are they?

He was surprised he could hear her so well through the din. He shook his head no.

What did you see? Tell me.

He looked at her and shrugged. Vampires, he said.

She nodded and took a sip from her glass.[12]

---

12 Where the Nazi photographs are overt and obvious, full of pomp, horror and history, Carell's photos are classical, traditional and subtle to the point of erasure. Not only is little attention paid to fixing the images to time and space, but there is also almost no attention paid to the aesthetic quality of the images. Just as there is nothing to fix the subject in any historical context, there is likewise no technical gesture to fix the image in any artistic or aesthetic context. These are images and aesthetic choices, seemingly without history. It goes without saying they contain no critique.

On the one hand, for all their banality, for all their transparency, the images are not innocuous. It's not that they work to glamorize fascism because, with few exceptions, the subjects, while elite and obviously affluent, are so generalized, so anonymous, that the images become strangely non-aspirational. There are simply not enough outstanding details in her photos for the viewer to latch onto, to latch onto and desire. Even when the subject is recognizable, as with the portrait of Luchino Visconti (figure 10) or one of the Mussolinis, the portraits do nothing to suggest that the lives are either approachable, exemplary, or enviable in any way. The problem is not the glamorization of fascism but the naturalization of it.

Let us be absolutely clear. Fascism, like all ideologies, is primarily a set of choices. When these choices are seen not as choices, but as somehow predetermined, natural, primordial conditions or "facts," then the set of choices becomes a set of givens, and true choice, true freedom, is eliminated. In some sense, then, the everyday portrait photographs of Ghitta Carell are infinitely more pernicious than the insane photography of Nazi Germany at its peak, in that Carell's work seeks to domesticate, and thereby mask, the insistence on racial hierarchy and obedience that forms the foundation, the non-choice, of fascism.

And yet.

Chapter 7
Martin Margiela, "The Photocopy Show"

Millie.

Mr. Dunn. Did you have any trouble getting here?

No. The Oval Café. I've never heard of it.

I would come here often, whenever I was in town. It used to be a fashion model's hangout, so many years ago. I don't know who comes here now. Please, sit down.

Thank you.

What would you like?

Just coffee.

Oh? You are in a hurry.

It's almost eleven. I've already had breakfast and it's too early for lunch.

I need something, if you don't mind.

Of course not. Timo sent some prints over, some images they'd like to use for the book. I thought you could describe them for me, what you were doing, what was going on in your life and in your head, and I'd record that, maybe take some notes, and then write up extended captions based on what you've told me. I'm not sure how coherent the narrative will be: I don't think coherence is what they want. Does that sound OK?

I suppose.

Do you mind if I record you?

If it's necessary.

I don't want to make any mistakes. We don't have to use all of these, and so if there are images you don't want to talk about, or if there are images that simply don't mean much to you, then we can just discard them. I didn't pick them, so I've no idea how important or obscure they might be.

Yes, I would like two eggs, sunny side up, and rye toast, please. And please, more coffee.

I'll just have coffee, thank you.

I have this mic, it hooks up to my laptop, and I'll just put it right here, OK? I'll write this in first person: I would use third, but first might be more immediate. I can always change it. Just talking to myself here. Check, check. Check check. The mic's working.

I see you survived the dance club.

My ears are still ringing, but otherwise, yeah. Should we get started?

By all means.

This has something written on the back. It looks like they all do. Margiela SS 1990. What does SS mean?

Spring Summer.

Any time you're ready.

This was my first show. I had only met Martin the day before. If I remember correctly, I was with my Aunt Sophie and we were walking by the *Lariboisière* hospital on the way from the train station to my aunt's flat. I had just flown in from Denver and was completely exhausted. I think Martin approached my aunt, or maybe it was Jenny,

Jenny Meirens, Martin's business partner; she died a couple of years ago. Anyway, one of them spoke to my aunt and asked if I had ever modeled before, and if I would like to. My aunt was skeptical, but Martin could be charming and so my aunt let them talk to me. I had enough French and they had enough English, and I thought why not? I remember Martin told me to wear jeans and keep my hair, I forget what French word he used, unkempt, messy, *en désordre* maybe.

I didn't know what to expect. The show was at this derelict playground, way out in the 20th *arrondissement*, near the cemetery. I didn't do a first look, a dress rehearsal; I'd only met them the day before. The neighborhood was impoverished, not quite *les banlieues*, but definitely poor. The playground was run-down: the sidewalks were cracked, the fences collapsed and there was garbage on the ground. People were everywhere, including a number of frolicking children. I was beginning to have second thoughts. I thought Martin was a student or something and I wasn't expecting such a crowd.

Jenny steered me to the dressing room, the dressing tent, before I could change my mind. Pure chaos. There were electrical cords and cables running every which way. It was cold, October, and they had portable heaters going full blast. A long rack of clothes ran against the far wall. There was hardly any light, and most of the lamps focused on the makeup chairs. I saw Martin walking around dressing the models with an assistant holding an ancient quartz lamp with a thick orange cord trailing behind. There weren't that many people working besides Martin and Jenny: maybe three or four others, plus Inge, the makeup artist and her two assistants. There must have been fifty models, fifty different looks. Some were dressed, some were almost naked, there were shoes and dresses strewn about everywhere, someone was yelling over the music; it was crazy. Everybody was freezing and huddling by these weak heaters.

The clothes were beautiful. I remember being enchanted by all the different dresses, jackets, skirts and what have you. That's what I remember most: the clothes took my breath away. Someone gave me a canvas bag to put my stuff in, and they led me to Martin, who brought me over to the rack and handed me this tweed skirt made from men's trousers. He then slipped a pretty white cotton dress over my shoulders and turned the top down over the skirt. It was nice. Strange, but nice. Martin motioned for me to take my bra off. I was a little flustered, especially when he brought out this metal vest, this breastplate, but I was *not* going to back out, so off came the bra and on came the solid metal vest. It wasn't terribly comfortable, this vest, it was heavy and cut into my shoulders. But I didn't care. It was fun. Scary but fun. I appreciated the contrast of how it all felt: the men's tweed skirt, the white cotton dress and the heavy metal vest.

I didn't have any shoes. They had boots for everyone, Tabi boots, but they ran out or they didn't have my size, didn't have my big American feet size, so I wore my own sneakers, my Converse sneakers. I was going to go out barefoot, but the catwalk was bare ground, gravel and sharp rocks and who knows, so they let me get my shoes from the bag. Inge did my makeup, white eye shadow, dark eyeliner and thick lashes, and she painted a 90 on my arm. Someone tousled up my hair for a bit, then Martin gave a long speech to the models about acting natural and not acting like models—I was surprised I understood most of it—and then he thanked us for all our help. Five minutes after that, the show started and five minutes after that they all gave me a quick once-over, mussed my hair again, and I walked through the curtain.

It was weird, having all those people looking at me, and all those cameras pointing at me. I know they were looking at the clothes, the metal vest, the dress used as a skirt and the underskirt made of pants, but still, I wasn't used to it. I liked it and didn't like it. It was a playground, with all these families and kids mixing with the fashion people, the journos and photographers. It was over so quickly, and then I circled back to the dressing tent, where we were all handed white lab coats to put over our clothes for the finale. We all walked at the end, even Martin, and that was it. Jenny found my bag of clothes and helped me change, and Martin asked me to come by the studio the next week, and I went back to my aunt's flat.

Did you ever model before that? Locally? In Colorado?

No, never.

Did you consider it?

It never crossed my mind. I was not interested in fashion before I walked in that show.

What were you interested in?

I played volleyball in high school because I was tall, and I studied Spanish and French in my first semester, my only semester, in college.

What happened after that?

I went to the atelier a week later. This was the one on Saint-Denis: he and Jenny painted it all white. Everything. . . .walls, furniture, ceiling, floor, all white. I didn't see Martin at first, just Jenny and Serge and maybe Benjamin. They were really depressed: the reviews had been terrible, and they weren't sure they wanted to keep the company going. Then Martin came in and he had a couple of bottles of wine in his arms. I thought he'd been drinking, and I was a little worried, but no, he was happy and wanted to celebrate. He asked Jenny, why are you so sad, and Jenny told him the reviews, they are terrible, and he said, don't worry, I know what I am doing. It was then that he asked me if I wanted to be his fit model. For some reason I agreed.

Why?

It was Paris. I wanted to see the world. I thought maybe I could save some money for college. I didn't know what fit model meant. I was only planning to do it for a year.

What did your parents think?

My mother was furious at my aunt, her sister, for snatching me out of school. That lasted a while. My father, I think he was confused by the whole thing. Later, when I started making a little money, he approved.

Everyone remembers their first time, right? I had just flown to Paris from Colorado and was extremely jet-lagged. My aunt and I were walking near the train station, and this charismatic man came up to my aunt and asked in French to speak to me. He was charming and polite, and said he was a clothing designer by the name of Martin Margiela, and would I like to model for him. Modelling? In Paris? Where do I sign up?

The show was the very next day. I was so excited I could hardly get to sleep that night. Me, a nobody from Walsenburg, Colorado, was going to model on a runway in Paris.

When we got to the playground where the show was to be held, my heart sank. First of all, it was in the outskirts of the city, in a sketchy neighborhood by a cemetery and secondly, it was at this derelict playground. It was the opposite of glamorous. So much for my sophisticated new career. I almost went back to my aunt's.

But I thought I might not get another chance. Somebody showed me the dressing room— it was actually a tent—and I couldn't believe my eyes. There were clothes everywhere, electrical cables all along the floor, girls with white eye shadow running around half naked, loud music and yelling. . . I wasn't in Colorado anymore, Toto.

But the clothes were gorgeous. Martin gave me my look: the base layer was a tweed skirt made of men's trousers. The covering layer was a pretty cotton dress turned down at the waist to form a skirt. And yes, on top was a breastplate made of iron, a vest of polished metal. Not the most comfortable top, but it was striking.

It was a blast. I remember just before I was to walk, Martin told me that he didn't want me to look like a model; he wanted me to look like the beautiful girl that I was. That really meant everything to me. How could I go wrong? I walked out through the curtain, and I could hear the cameras clicking away and feel the people all looking at me and I was thrilled. This is what I wanted to do. This is where I belonged. I vowed right then that I would do anything to make my dream come true. The next week, Martin hired me to work in his studio full-time.

This was the beginning of a beautiful relationship.

Margiela FW 1995. That's a big jump. Do you want to find an image closer to 1990?

The Red Show, that's what they called it. I always thought of it as the Circus Show. I don't know how chronological you want this to be.

Go ahead. I can always re-arrange the order. I'll ask Timo what kind of chronology they want. Are we sure that's even you?

Oh, because of the mask? Yeah, that's me. I remember the outfit: denim jacket, red velvet dress, black tights, painted red Tabis. Everything in the show was either some shade of red or dark brown or black. And we all wore those masks. Until the finale at the end.

That's not a leather jacket?

No, it was painted denim. This was not my favorite show.

Why not?

First of all, it was held at a real circus out in the 16th. Real big-top, real animals, real circus smells. The animals were off to the side, and their odor was everywhere. I don't mind animal smells, but it was raining like hell, which produced wet animal smells. I could have done without the rain and the mud. And the fact that the show started two hours late, so there was a lot of sitting around. What else? The catwalk was really narrow, and we had to do a circuit around the audience who were sitting in risers, bleachers. Bleachers with stairs. And we were wearing those masks. It wasn't impossible to see through the nylon with our faces covered, but it wasn't that easy. And I didn't love the clothes. Remember, I was his fit model, so I had worn all of the looks before, and while I don't mind a limited palette, the overall designs weren't nearly as interesting as most of his other shows. At least not to me.

What did you think? About wearing the mask?

I had worn masks earlier, but that was the first time we all did it. Like I said, it was hard to see. Martin wanted the clothes to be what everyone looked at, concentrated on. He didn't want anything getting in the way of the clothes. That's why, after the first couple of years, he never came out in the finale, never did interviews, never got photographed.

What else can you add? Anything personal? What was going on in your life at the time?

Is this necessary?

The more detail I have, the more three-dimensional you'll be. The rest of the book will focus on Margiela, his shows, his clothes. This chapter is about you. What did it feel like to wear that mask, for instance? What was different about it?

You mentioned making me more three-dimensional. That's exactly what I was for, as a fit model, to be three-dimensional, to be a body that would allow the clothes to exist in space, to enable Martin to move from *croquis* to *toiles* to actual garments, which would then become the clothes women would wear in their lives. I was even four-dimensional when I walked, when I moved, when I moved with the clothes in time through space, because that's what fashion modeling is. Adding dimensions to what were once merely ideas. Or dreams, even.

I loved wearing the mask. On the one hand, the mask made us even more faceless, more mechanical, more of a tool or device. We were purer somehow, a pure tool for displaying the clothes. On the other hand, since no one could see our faces, we could smile, laugh, stick our tongues out, stare back at someone, stare back at all those eyes staring at us. The masks made me more ambivalent, Mr. Dunn, which is to say, more human. I see that you don't understand. Anyway, we were wearing full makeup under the masks. That was a bit strange. We came out in the finale in full makeup, carrying red balloons.

What else happened to you in 1995?

Do you remember what you were doing in 1995?

I was in grad school. With Timo.

Half a lifetime ago. Some of it's hard to place, what year I did what. I went to Italy in 1995, I remember because it was a couple of weeks after this show. I walked for Martin in Milan in February or March, and then I did some fit work at the knitwear company, the mills, Miss Deanna. I holidayed with some friends down in Rome, where we rode vespas, ate gelato, listened to Madonna, and I learned to drink Negronis. One of the women I was with, Geneviève, knew a photographer who lived there, so we crashed for a couple of weeks at his villa. How could these clichés be of interest to anyone, Mr. Dunn?

You don't think life-stories are interesting?

Lives are interesting. While you live them. I'm suspicious of life-stories.

Why?

I distrust the language. And the form. I tried keeping a journal while I was in high school, but I never could find the right words to describe what happened to me. The words I wrote always distorted whatever I did. And the idea that life has form, that it develops into some kind of story, I think that's ludicrous. Life has no story. Life *is* no story.

The Red Show, or as I like to call it, the Circus Show. It was a circus in more ways than one, for sure. Let me try to set the scene for you. Imagine a real circus tent, a big-top on the outskirts of Paris. Now imagine that the animals, the elephants and tigers and all, are all living, eating and whatever, in the next tent. Now imagine a heavy rainstorm that started early in the morning. Can you guess where I'm going with this? Imagine how your dog smells when wet, then multiply that by ten. Now put on a full nylon mask, one you can see through, but with difficulty. Now turn some of the lights off and try to walk on a narrow band circling the outside of the main ring. Now walk up and down stairs, and circle through a crowd sitting on bleachers. Now try to do this a day after you've broken up with your boyfriend of over a year after he's moved to Canada. That was the Red Show to me.

After the Red Show, I traveled to Rome with my friends. We rode vespas, ate gelato, drank Negronis and crashed at this photographer's villa near a beach. The Red Show faded into a distant memory. So did the boy.

Do you see the jacket? It's not red leather; it's painted blue denim. I still have it. It's aging beautifully.

What about this one? There's nothing written except a date, 1998.

Oh dear. That's Stella, Stella Tennant. And me, obviously. On the shoot she did with Mark Borthwick. She was so gorgeous.

I don't know who this is.

Stella Tennant was a famous model: not a supermodel, but not far off. She was British royalty, related to some duke or something. We didn't work together much: our basic look was too similar, perhaps, but I always liked hanging out with her. She was kind, funny, generous and smart, one of the truly beautiful people in fashion. I miss her.

What happened?

She died last year.

From COVID?

Yeah. Well, no. I don't want to talk about her. Please don't use this picture. Let's go to the next.

You can meet truly beautiful people in fashion, truly generous souls who shine through the darkness and make our lives a little brighter. Rest in Power, Stella Tennant.

Von Unwerth 2001.

That's me trying to look sexy. I was getting old and I was probably high. These were not my salad days.

Oh?

Look how much foundation I'm wearing: I look like a clown. Drugs made my skin blotchy and pimply, hence the near pancake. You can't tell from this photo, but I'm like 98 pounds here.

Who's that with you?

You mean whose boob am I kissing? The exquisite breast of one Deirdre Jensen. We did some jobs together. She was a friend. Still is. This was all her idea. She and Ellen, Ellen Von Unwerth, the photographer, went way back. I don't remember much about that shoot at all. Like I said, I was high. I do think Dierdre was trying to pull me out of my junk funk. She and Ellen thought that maybe a little whimsy would help. It didn't.

Can you tell me anything more about your drug use?

Surely you know the rhythm of addiction, Mr. Dunn.

Can you elaborate?

I used drugs consistently from 2001 to 2003. Then I quit.

Your addiction affected your modeling life, yes? So it might be useful to include some details. I'd like to hear your particulars.

Junk stories are all the same. One of two possible endings.

You agreed to cooperate.

I first started taking drugs in 2000. In 2001, I took drugs consistently, but perhaps wasn't truly addicted until that winter. I quit, or rather was replaced as Martin's fit model at the end of '99 because Martin wanted a change. I had some trouble finding work after that for a while: I've never been that comfortable going to look-sees, and perhaps that had something to do with it all. And I was bored, I suppose. In the beginning, I managed to clean up enough for gigs I did get, but that didn't last; I lost weight and my skin got bad, so I stopped showing up. In 2002, I began to run out of money and was living in circumstances which were, let's just say, unfortunate. Martin found out and somehow got me the gig at Hermès. In the beginning, they only used my face, as I still weighed under a hundred pounds. A few months and a few quiches later, I filled out enough so they could do full shots. I tried not to live in Paris: I moved to New York and came to Paris only as necessary. After a year my contract with Hermès wasn't renewed, mutually wasn't renewed, in 2003. I didn't do much modeling after that: a few things for Martin, a few things for Rei, but my heart wasn't in it, and I was over thirty, which was fine for Hermès but not so much for Rei's *karasu* kids. I had made enough money from Hermès to retire, so I did.

Were you busted in Britain?

You've done your homework, I was, but they let me go. Have no idea why.

Did you ever go to any clinic or anything?

What did Amy sing? No, no, no.

This might look like a glamorous, sexy photograph, but I can tell you that it's not. It's not because I don't remember taking it. I don't remember taking it because I was high on various drugs much of the time between 2001 and 2003. Most of the drugs I used made sex and sexiness impossible, or at least terribly beside the point.

I'm not going to preach, and I'm not going to lie. And I'm certainly not going to judge. But here's my story.

Modeling is hard work. I always knew that. But there are two things I wish someone had told me about the modeling life. #1 EVERYONE GETS REJECTED and #2 EVERYONE

GETS BORED. We all know rejection sucks, but in my case, after I left Margiela's studio, I had a couple of bookings I didn't get, and those self-image questions began to spiral: Are I too skinny? Am I not busty enough? Is my neck too long? Should I change my hair color? Wear my hair longer? Shorter? Should I try for a more natural look? Etc. etc. etc. I didn't handle it well.

Also, they never tell you about the boredom. If you're not getting gigs, there are only so many hours of each day you can spend at the gym and shopping. And back when I was working, the gym wasn't necessarily the first place I went in the morning. So the days got longer and longer. Another thing they don't tell you is how boring the shoots themselves can be. No matter how tremendous the photographer or how fabulous the location, there will be down time. There's a lot of work to be done in order to get you, the model, looking just right. And Rome wasn't built in a day. Makeup alone can take hours of simply sitting still. I didn't handle that well either.

I started to show up a little high for the jobs I was hired for, then a little higher, and then I stopped showing up, and then I stopped getting hired.

It also didn't help that the man I was seeing at the time was, should we say, an expert in scoring: he could get anything he wanted. And I mean anything. Dude's drug game was on point. I am not going to blame anyone else, but drugs started to become readily available. And I seemed to have the time.

I don't remember much of 2001. I had gigs; there's pho-

tographic evidence, but I honestly can't recall many details. Much of what I do remember—bruises from sleeping on a stone floor, craving something, anything on the interminable plane ride from Paris to New York, losing a gig at Versace because I was too skinny—isn't very pleasant or inspiring.

My friends, my friends saved me. I won't embarrass them by naming names, but if it weren't for them, I wouldn't be here now. One more thing I remember. During the worst of it, the times I was ready to throw in the towel, I kept hearing Madonna's "Die Another Day"; I heard that song everywhere. "There's so much more to know/I guess I'll die another day/ It's not my time to go." So yeah, I survived.

Hermès 2002 FW

I'm skinny, *tres décharmé*, there, I can tell. When I was this thin, they'd put me in all these scarves and jackets and loose-fitting clothes that Martin was doing anyway. I liked wearing Hermès. The material was exquisite, all soft wool, cashmere and vicuña even. Here, let me look, that's a dark lambswool coat, with a cashmere *vareuse* shirt and a grey skirt, I'm guessing cashmere as well. I still have the lambswool coat. I think that's a vicuña scarf.

The best part about modeling was wearing the clothes, feeling the material on my skin, appreciating all the work that had gone into the choices made in the design and the expertise in the execution, and enjoying how all that made me feel. I didn't care if anyone looked at me or not: I understood how absolutely breathtaking the clothes were.

Being looked at was somewhat of an intrusion.

Actually, that's not completely true. When I really like things, like this Hermès lambswool jacket, I do want others to see them: not to see me, but to see the clothes. And if I have to get dressed and made up so that the clothes can be seen, well, what of it? I guess I never did reconcile my shyness with my desire to show off the clothes.

After the drugs, it took me a while to get back into modeling shape. The drugs did a number on my body. I've always been skinny, but if the drugs tell you not to eat for days at a time, you get downright scrawny. Turns out, you can be too thin.

So here I am, clean and sober but still thin as a stick. Hence the baggy clothes. Or should I say that everything looked baggy on me?

I've always loved Hermès. I loved wearing the clothes, feeling the material on my skin and appreciating all the work that had gone into the design and the craftsmanship. To me, that's the best part about modeling. It's like having my personal piece of art always with me. A piece of art I can touch.

Hermès 24 *Faubourg Vogue* October 1999. They are out of order.

I remember that shoot. That shoot was fun. The Palace of Versailles, I think it was the Queen's bedroom, the one next to the Hall of Mirrors. I forget who the photographer was; it wasn't anyone I'd worked with before, but he kept telling me to swoon. Swoon, Miss Del'Aria, swoon please. At first, I wasn't sure I was hearing him right, but then I just really liked the way he said it. Swoon, swoon. So I swooned.

You're not wearing any clothes. Just flowers.

I'm wearing a belt. And I'm wearing the perfume, *Calèche*. The belt is Barenia leather. I still have it; I wore it the other day.

You're blonde here.

It was a wig. Look at my thigh there, I almost have an ass. I'm nearly plump.

Did you do nudes often?

I wouldn't call that a nude. You can't really see anything.

That's not an answer.

Yes and no. How's that?

Were you ever married?

And that is your business how?

This is a chapter about your life. Family, marriage, children, all part of your life.

This chapter is about my *modeling* life. My so-called career.

One's family affects one's career, don't you think? I know mine does. I've dedicated my first book to my wife, and I've thanked her profusely in all. My writing would be very different if we'd not met or married. Or not had children.

So you think. No, never married.

Do you have children?

No. And no cats either, if that's your next question.

But your sister lives with you?

She does. But I've nothing more to say about her or any of my family.

Were you ever almost married?

Once. When I was thirty-seven, thirty-eight? Thirty-seven. Regardless, some years after I retired.

When you were modeling, did you have a serious, um, partner?

One or two, I suppose. Two or three. Depends on what you mean by serious.

Exclusive?

When I first moved to Paris I met a man, a boy my age, who worked in a bookstore, and we were exclusive for about a year, until he went to university in Canada. He was into Foucault, if memory serves. There were a couple of others. There was a sleazy Belgian man whom I lived with for a time when I was doing drugs, but when I quit drugs I had to quit him; otherwise I never would have quit drugs. There were others.

Less serious?

Not necessarily.

Can I get names?

No. You'll have to make them up.

Do any of these relationships correspond to the photos we're looking at?

I had just broken up with bookstore boy before the

Circus Show. The trip to Italy had been a rebound holiday. I was likely living with the Belge during the Unwerth shoot, although, like I said, I don't remember well enough to be sure. But in 2001, it was likely.

Here I am, wearing only flowers, a belt and a smile. And perfume. And a wig. My skin color doesn't usually go with blonde hair, but here, it just seemed right. That photo was taken at the Palace of Versailles, in the Queen's bedroom next to the Hall of Mirrors. The photographer, I forget his name, kept telling me to swoon, swoon. So here I am, swooning away.

I was happy here, plump and happy. My head was in a good space; my career was going well, I had a lot of friends and I was travelling (and I must have been eating). But you never can tell when things are going to change. You have to enjoy life while you can.

I hardly ever do nudes, by the way. I like wearing clothes too much.

Comme des Garcons, SS 2003

I think this was my last gig. At least my last official show. I walked in Martin's show in February and then did a few shoots during the summer, and then, *voilà*, the finale.

I walked the show in Paris, then Rei flew me to Tokyo for fashion week, which is where this photo was taken. There I am, desperately holding the jacket over my belly to cover my boob. That's my expression of intense concentration, in case you're wondering. The undershirt was black pinstripe, like from a man's suit. The seams were raw, as you can see, and there were no fasteners, no buttons or clasps or anything. Just my hand. The next layer, the white blouse, was silky cotton, but again, nothing to hold it together. The linen vest was somehow cut so it appeared to be two different layers, but with no fasteners. Exquisite tailoring, and I like all those layers, how they flow and move. Rei insisted I put my hands in my pockets before I walked, so there I am, trying to pinch the pockets in over my navel so my boob doesn't flop out. I think that's the only time I've ever worn harem pants, before or since. It's just not a look I fancy. I do like those ballet flats though. I have no comment on whatever it is that's on my head.

Why did you decide to retire?

It was time. Even though I had moved back to Paris, the Hermès schedule was demanding, plus I got the feeling that they'd prefer someone more well-known and easier to work with. More bankable and more malleable. And I didn't want to fuck anything up for Martin: he'd gone out on a limb for me once, and I didn't want to have him have to do it again. And I possessed mirrors, Mr. Dunn. I could see the laugh lines settling, the crow's feet expanding, brows beginning to harden into the scowl you see today. And, well, it was never my goal to be *une mannequin, de cabine* or otherwise. I wanted to do other things.

Such as?

I considered moving to Japan, actually. Rei brought me over early before the shoot; she wanted me to relax or something, so she set me up in a country *ryokan*, a traditional inn outside of a cluster of hot springs. Kaga was the name of the village. There's little to do but soak in the springs, eat and look at the leaves on the trees. I loved it. No one spoke English, I didn't have any books, and I was silent much of the time, like a monk. Every day at dinner, the hostess would bring out a variety of dishes, small plates, and meticulously describe every dish to me in some detail. In Japanese. She didn't speak English and knew I spoke no Japanese, but still she took her time to explain, as best she could, what it was I was going to eat. There was a real respect there, for me as a guest, as well as for the food.

I remember one evening after a long bath, I was walking in the gardens, my breath visible in the cool air, when I heard the faintest sound of a low-pitched flute. It sounded like it could have been the wind, but it was too purposeful, too persistent. I decided to try to find the source, just to make sure it wasn't a breeze blowing through something or other, or the manifestation of some desire on my part. I turned to follow a path I wasn't familiar with, and while I thought I must have been moving closer to the source, it wasn't getting any more distinct or certain. I was about to give up and turn back when I noticed this rustling behind some bushes, and I saw what appeared to be a chubby little fox running around a copse of trees. It noticed me and stopped, looked me over, and then began to jog down a narrow trail to my right, glancing over its shoulder as if it wanted me to follow. Which I did. The flute music remained just on this side of my perception, and I followed the fox's curly cream-colored tail up the side of a hill, over a stream and through a small meadow. The colors, blues and greens, with some wisps of silver and purple, were magical. Not vivid or bright, but subtle and essential somehow, right, profound. I don't have the language. The fox would turn its head every so often to make sure I was behind, to make sure I was noticing the beauty around us, and then continue on, its little ass sashaying along. A vista opened, and what appeared to be silvery clouds floated over the horizon, suspended in the sky. At a closer glance I saw that these were snow caps of distant hills reflecting the scattered moonlight. It was all glorious, fairylike even, in the darkening light. The darkness grew and became almost total, and I started to worry about finding my way back. Suddenly, we turned abruptly and almost burst through a stone gate, the back garden of my inn, a few steps from where I had started. The flute music stopped abruptly, and a young woman, a teenager, came out of the door and greeted the fox, which, it turned out, was the family dog, a small Akita, a Shiba Inu. Kita was her name. I learned later that foxes seldom have curly tails and that their snouts are more elongated, so it was never a fox. I never heard the flute again. I've never told anyone that story before.

But you didn't move there?

No. Family was always an issue, plus the language barrier was real. And Tokyo is expensive. I owned my flat in Paris and didn't think I could get something comparable in Tokyo or Osaka. Let's move on, shall we?

This was from my last show, in Japan. The end of my career.

It was time to retire. I was clean and sober and ready for the next chapter of my life. I had accomplished everything I wanted to as a fashion model: I'd made a good living, had travelled the world, met creative and sometimes brilliant people, and collected more than a few beautiful clothes.

For a while, I thought the next chapter might take place in Japan. I spent some time in a ryokan, a traditional inn near hot springs in the village of Kaga. I spent most of the time in meditation and walks in the gardens. No one spoke English and I didn't speak Japanese, so I lived like a monk, alone with my thoughts. One night, as I was walking near the inn, I saw a fox who began to trot ahead of me, looking back to signal that I was to follow. I did, and she took me through a strange and wondrous path, full of dark, deep purples and perfect blues contrasting with silver wisps in the darkening sky. It was indescribably beautiful. We came upon a vista where silver clouds seemed suspended against the black horizon. Even now, I get a little emotional just thinking about it. It was getting dark, and I felt like I should turn back and try to make my way back to the inn when we turned a corner sharply and almost stumbled through this old wooden gate and came to the back garden of my inn, the place where I had started some time before. It was indeed a magical night.

So yes, I've always had a soft spot for Japan, and I return any chance I get.

CHAPTER 8
MARTIN MARGIELA,
"THE 20TH ANNIVERSARY SHOW"

The bad news was that her flight was canceled. Something about a sick crew and sick replacements. The good news was that somehow Timo had managed to bump her up to business for the midnight flight, a mere three hours hence. Further, as she was informed by the tired woman at the counter, the Air France Business Class Lounge had just re-opened the day before, masks of course required. She had a couple of *policiers*, Fred Vargas and Elizabeth Wilson, but decided on the purchase of an American *Vogue* at the rapidly closing magazine store, cover featuring an awkwardly posed Charlize Theron in something sheer and polka-dotted. Her marked indifference to both Theron and the cover-promised New Scottish Gardens perhaps made the buy possible, as anything less irrelevant might border on the masochistic. She wanted distraction from the impending recollecting and reliving of the recent New York Golden Oldies experience and was afraid that actual reading would be impossible. Plus, her contacts were bothering her. She would thumb through the glossy pages, maybe with a glass of champagne, and hope that the rapid succession of consumer images and/or faded personal associations would keep the more recent memories at bay.

And maybe with just the one glass of champagne. She had drunk too freely during the six days in New York, and although the night of the rooftop party had been the nadir, the entire trip had been a constant if shallow descent into inelegance and self-pity. She had thrown her cigarettes away in the morning and was now hungry, although she also felt a bit bloated and sluggish from the accumulation of alcohol, lack of sleep and irritation of having to deal with people and surroundings simultaneously strange and familiar. Mostly, she was depressed.

The lounge was relatively easy to find and nearly empty, with a young couple staring into phones near the window and a family of four quietly filling plates at the buffet. She sat heavily in the furthest corner from the entrance, her back against the window, removed her Max Mara coat and placed her Hermès Grey Picotin on the chair next to her. She owned a Birken but never travelled with it, having had one stolen in London by a friend of Cocaine Kate's at a drug party at Issy Blow's house somewhere in the British countryside. She hadn't known Kate well, at all, really, but remained astounded to this day at her capacity to consume everything except food. That was a story Dunn would like, full of celebrities (at the time), drugs and sex. Not that she could remember much: she had arrived with Sonia, her Birken and a change of clothes and had left three days later without anything save her skirt, her shoes and someone's Marks and Spencer peasant top. That London scene was too much, there was always death about, a guest consistently invited. She was never interested, much preferring the louche lethargy of her Parisian heroin cohort to the frantic eschatology of the Brits. But that was all so long ago.

She took her *Vogue* out of the Picotin but left it unopened on the table. She checked her phone—a couple of emails, three new texts—and returned it to the pocket of her jacket. She looked around in her bag, found her air pods and fiddled with them, then returned them to their case. She felt hot and took her coat off. *One* glass of champagne and a piece of bread and cheese, but she remained in her seat, the fingers of her right hand (nails self-done and short, painted a matte grey with a touch of lavender) drumming on the table. The family of four was sitting across the room in her line of sight. The mother, a round brunette, was fussing with the kids and their plates while the father, she assumed, sat slouched and unconcerned, studying his phone and drinking his beer.

She'd gotten up late and had breakfasted around noon, her traditional bowl of oatmeal and an apple with coffee. She'd had a plate of cold white grapes around four, the fruit less flavorful than it appeared, but nothing since, and she could feel her stomach tightening. She would feel better if she ate, and it would give something to occupy her hands and her thoughts. But she sat still, hesitating as if paralyzed or bound, her fingers audible on the table, her eyes resting on the large blue, red and white mural of *Le Coq Gallois* on the far wall.

OK. She shook her head once and quieted her fingers. She got up from the chair and began to make her way over to the buffet table. The father looked up from his phone and kept looking as she moved deliberately across the room. She could feel his look on the skin of the back of her shoulder blades, her ass, the back of her knees. She bristled.

Beef Bourgogne, haricots verts amandine, a selection of *pain et fromage, ratatouille,* an unnamed quiche, and a selection of various mousse and puddings. She found a large white plate and took half of a ladle of ratatouille, then two pieces of bread and a small piece of Roquefort. Was this too much food? She turned to the wine cart, with a large tub of ice holding an opened bottle of *Lenoble Blanc de Blanc* and a corked bottle of *Albert Bichot Bourgogne Aligoté* among assorted reds and liquors. She set her plate down and poured herself a glass of the Blanc de Blancs, filling it almost to the rim. She spilled a little as she gathered silverware and walked back, the wine sloshing on her fingers on the stem. She could see her reflection in the darkened window but dropped her eyes quickly. She set it all down, turned and sat, and immediately looked over to the man who had been staring. He was nowhere to be seen, his chair vacant, his family eating quietly and earnestly in his absence.

She put her napkin on her lap, removed her mask and took a bite of the ratatouille. Not bad, although it could use a little more garlic. The wine was good and cold. Another couple, middle-aged men, entered and sat a few tables to her left, and a young blonde with a severe pixie cut, dressed in a denim skirt and jacket, walked in with a three-legged Sheltie and sat in the middle of the room to her right against the window. The Sheltie turned once or twice and curled at her mistress' feet.

The father, in a maroon Adidas tracksuit, returned to his family, said something to the mother, rubbed the head of one of his kids, then sat down and looked directly at her. He wasn't wearing a mask. She stopped eating to meet his gaze, although the distance was too great to ensure they were actually making eye contact. He continued staring for a while until finally he took a drink of his beer and looked away to his phone. She turned to her bread and cheese.

Her heart was beating quickly. What was he looking at? She'd tried to dress, if not anonymously then unobtrusively, with regular cut Levi's Made in Japan, a *marinière* from Saint James and Cydwoq flats. Her beige Max Mara cashmere coat provided protection, but it was folded on the chair next to her. She'd barely combed her hair and had bags under her eyes that two afternoon teabags couldn't erase. It couldn't have been the extra bright lipstick she'd put on to distract from her overserved pores or her Tiffany cat earrings with the diamond eyes Robert had given her for her birthday, as the separating distance precluded the observation of such detail. She'd considered going full burqa, combining oversized Dries sunglasses with an N95, scarf (Cucinelli?) and a turtleneck, but that look tended to attract more than deflect and she was almost sweating in her *marinière* as it was.

Who was he looking at? Was she merely the random woman, her salience traceable to her very existence? Was his ogling habitual, restlessly fastening upon all and sundry, or could her visibility be traced to her differing from the familial? Or was there something distinctive he saw, some detail he noticed that caused him to look again, to focus and then to shamelessly stare? With or without specificity, his attention was impersonal and fleeting, surely, just as surely as hers was not. That unfairness rankled.

She had this fantasy of wearing a full-length gown made of mirrors so that anyone looking at her would see nothing but their own reflection. They would see nothing but their reflection looking at their reflection, so that jerk dad over there would see nothing but a thirty-something jerk dad in a maroon track suit, a pumpkin-colored tee shirt and a scraggly beard looking at a thirty-something jerk dad in a maroon track suit, etc.

This was more or less what had happened when she took Jonathan to the club.

The Roquefort was sharp and musty tasting, surprisingly good. The wine went down easily.

Neither the prolonged gaze (his) nor the accompanying deliberation (hers) was novel or unique: this was the sea in which she swam and had been swimming since she was fifteen or so. His stare had been visceral, an unwelcome and callused caress, and it had made her feel conspicuous and vulnerable. Her skin was now charged, hypersensitive, attuned to the smallest vibration of attention, ambient or not. This wasn't always the reaction: often she shrugged it off, disregarded or accepted it, granted it a first but not a second thought. This was not to say that she ever could ignore it, for she could not—the aggressive eye always registered somewhere—but it was to suggest that it didn't always upset or preoccupy her mind and it didn't always put her body on red alert.

She closed her lips and constricted her throat to begin her slow *ujjayi* breathing. She hadn't done any yoga for her six days in New York, partly due to irregular hours but mostly due to an attack of childish petulance. Soon after she arrived, she could feel the trip disappoint, so had decided to avoid any activity that might mitigate the frustration. Her instinct, her body had resisted participation in the book project from the beginning, and she should have listened and stayed out. Stayed home. The smoking, drinking, bad eating and just general bad behavior had been both penance and indulgence, and the annoyance and irritation she now felt over that lingering gaze was partially a reaction to that.

She breathed in and out, in and out, and felt herself calming. She opened her eyes slowly and turned to look over at the three-legged dog, curled at its master's feet. That was the life, sleeping and self-contained, largely impervious to the attention of others. But such autonomy depended on the presence of a master, or at least, what were they called today, companions, yes, companions. The strays she noticed around Paris, both cats and dogs, seemed well-attuned to the vagaries of strangers. Did easy autonomy depend on someone to feed you? She had companions, she supposed; at least she had them before the pandemic. No masters. She didn't care to examine the metaphor too closely. She continued her pranayama breathing. Through her nose, the ocean.

She took another drink of champagne and another bite of cheese.

A pack of three twenty-something women giggled in, loud and American, and moved noisily behind a partition near the center of the room, thankfully out of her sight-line. An older couple followed, French or African, he in a nice YSL suit and she in a beautiful brick and choco-late Kente print multi-layered gown. They moved slowly, gracefully, almost as if underwater, and sat to the right of the dog and her companion. She looked closer at the dog's owner and saw that what she had initially thought was a skirt was, in fact, wide-legged jeans, JNCOs even. Jesus, she hated those pants. She wondered if they were new, making a comeback, or if the woman shopped vintage. She usually welcomed the churn of fashion and the reference or reappearance of styles and trends, but she really hoped that JNCOs remained buried in the obscurity of history. She disliked (and hadn't dressed for) Martin's 2000 Fall Winter, with his oversized everything, although his tai-lored size 70 something slacks with the fabric tucked and folded were gorgeous compared to those misshapen balloon-like jeans, trousers she'd not be caught dead in.

She took this all seriously. Maybe that was her trouble; she took her clothes seriously, personally. Not fashion, that was too general, but clothing, her clothing, her clothes, the actual garments she wore. While she didn't get angry about what other people wore, the choices they made, she did judge: she simply couldn't fathom the consciousness that would find those JNCOs aesthetically pleasing. There was no need to wear such atrocious pants when a good and inexpensive jean skirt by Chloé, Fleur du Mal or even Balzac would be infinitely more flattering. Fuck, even the Gap. She was disappointed, sorrowful was a better word, when she saw ugly or unthought outfits: people, if they took the time, had so much more choice than their outfits suggested. Perhaps she was no better than those fashion gods she despised: the bookers, editors and just general snobs who judged everything on first impressions and immediate appearance, and whose vision was so fucking limited and conservative.

No, she was better.

She thought of Timo and chuckled. She was quite fond of Timo—sweet and generous Timo—but he was really full of shit. His idea of fashion as ethics, what she could remember of it, was all well and good when people dressed smartly, but what about when people didn't, or tried and failed? Which was most people most of the time. They became invisible at best and subject to ridicule and disdain at worst. Like the slightly overweight woman who worked at her favorite patisserie, *Le Pain et La Rire,* who was convinced that high wedgies, tight jeans, and tighter cable knits were somehow a good look on her. She was from Brussels, not Paris. Or Sylvan, whom she stopped seeing partly (mostly) because he saw him wearing Birkenstocks once or twice (once when she ran into him accidently at the grocers). That was no ethical relationship, no letting the other be other, no love. There was judgment, disdain and contempt (maybe). They might be human, but they were less human than she was, less worthy somehow. Fashion separated into those who could dress well, those who had the knowledge, physique and means, and those who did not. Such fashion had beauty and possibilities, yes, but never love.

That wasn't completely true either. Timo was giving, Rei had always been solicitous *to her* (although her impatience and refusal to suffer fools could be misconstrued as meanness), and she'd never met anyone as loving as Stella had been. And everyone at the atelier, from Martin on down, had always been kind and generous. But there were assholes: vicious, competitive models; jealous, backbiting hair and makeup people; manipulative, predatory photographers; cruel and avaricious bookers; self-centered and egomaniacal designers. . . the list went on. And if you added drugs, money and sex to the asshole mix, the contrast between the most exquisite physical beauty and the most sordid brutality would make your head spin and your stomach empty.

She took a long drink of champagne and let the bubbles tickle her nose.

She had little room to talk about Timo after her own absurd mini-meltdown later that evening. Her aversion to the word girl was sincere and long-lived, but she had no reason to rave at Timo and Jonathan, two men she barely knew and who, as far as she knew, had little to do with the corruption of the term into its current fallen and fraught state. Even while in full rant mode, she'd felt aghast at how shrill and humorless she sounded, the stereotypical bitter spinster railing against men and their joy. She wasn't wrong about the word: in her ear it was always hateful shorthand for a host of sexist attitudes and behaviors and it irritated to no end how women in the industry readily accepted and embraced the noun and all the baggage it carried. But somehow, the gin and a hangover from her habitual solitude, pandemic and pre, had loosened her tongue and her customary discretion and she performed crassly and clumsily to an uncomprehending and embarrassed audience. She mistrusted words and girl was the worst of them. But still.

Timo she'd known for a while, as they shared a few acquaintances and a few fashion week cocktail party conversations back in the day. But Jonathan Dunn undoubtedly thought her a spoiled fashion bitch, unavailable and unfamiliar with either the so-called real or so-called intellectual worlds he believed he inhabited. In his eyes she was insubstantial, airy and weightless, pure surface like photographic paper, devoid of anything but the most trivial, immediate and superficial reactions. She had aged out of any use or purpose and was now a parasite, a gadfly with only sad traces of her previous decorative and/or fuckable functionality. Timo was right about one thing: Dunn was a priest of resentment, with his black crow outfit and his inescapable gassy odor of Torquemada judgment. He was like the far too many men she had known who pretended to be too busy, too deep and too soulful to care about what they wore or how they looked. Men for whom dressing up was a clean tee shirt or a change of socks, or men who wore the same fucking thing day after day, some combination of black and grey pants and black and grey shirts, the wardrobe chosen with the express purpose of never requiring anything but the smallest of decisions.

Clothes were personal. Her clothes were personal. She always remembered the first time she tried on new garments. She remembered when she bought the Max Mara long coat on sale at *Leclaireur Hérold* and being smitten by the weight of the drape (solid but not too heavy) as well as the golden rust color of the lining. She remembered opening the package and trying her Dior Chelsea boots on Christmas morning four years ago, a present from her sister Agnes, and being relieved when they fit (Agnes was terrific at gifts but hit or miss on sizes). The Japanese Denim Levi's were an emergency purchase (she'd accidentally left her Sézane Brut jeans at home) a few days before at the Levi's store in Hudson Yards. She'd been surprised about how soft they had felt when she tried them on. She'd also been surprised about how churlish the young clerk had been, whose mask stubbornly remained stuck underneath her nose.

Although the initial encounter with her clothing was remarkable, she could also recall, with extensive detail, what she had been wearing when important and sometimes not so important things had happened to her. She remembered quite well the charcoal Givenchy blazer with the white selvedge oxford dress shirt and high waisted electric blue Alexander McQueen cigarette pants she'd worn when she'd broken up with Robert in some tourist café near the Trocadero. She recalled the softness of the lapel as it brushed against her neck as she fought back tears as she explained her decision to leave. She also could remember the black Burberry raincoat she'd worn over the black wool Hermès dress with the barrel sleeves and Prada flats that she'd worn to her father's funeral on a crisp April day, her hands buried deep in the Burberry's pockets. She recalled the way her black Comme des Garcons sleeveless cutout dress, one hundred percent polyester and light as gossamer, floated slowly off her shoulders and down to the polished wooden floor in Rui's bedroom, his eyes glittering with desire. Or the cut-off Levi's, cropped Versace top with red Prada sandals she sported on a beach whose name she couldn't remember somewhere near the Spanish border. She was in her mid-thirties, after drugs and between men, and had gone south with Agnes, Agnes' boyfriend Charles, and her friends Doré and Iris. She didn't remember much of the trip other than a long walk with Iris on the beach, drinking *roja* from the bottle just as the sun was setting, her jeans slung low, her sandals in her hand.

She rotated twenty or so pieces into and out of her closet for Spring/Summer and Fall/Winter, with a number of auxiliary, anonymous articles supplementing. She took exquisite care with her clothes, and rather than replace she'd repair, as she'd befriended one of the seamstresses from the Margiela atelier (now retired) and had cultivated a Tokyo tailor well versed in the techniques of *sashiko* and *boro*. Most of the garments she acquired while modeling were now long in the tooth, but if fashion was temporal style was timeless, and her clothes somehow seemed to last. She never sold anything and would retire unrepairable garments to the back of her closet, carefully folded in heavy plastic. For what reason she didn't know. This is where the aforementioned Comme des Garcons polyester cutout now resided: while it probably could stand another mend or two, buried within its folds—somewhat like the lock of McQueen's hair sewn into his dresses—were painful memories of her failed relationship with Rui. She never bought retail and relied on a sort of luxe ragpicking network to acquire a supply of new old stock, unworn garments three to fifteen years old.

She could also construct an achronological personal history according to garments, not events. Taking the

Saint James *marinière* for example, she could readily recall the time she'd worn it to an afternoon concert (Ravel and Satie) at *la Philharmonie* just before the pandemic; dinner (cassoulet) celebrating her friend Ramona's pregnancy with her husband Denis at Bistro Paul Bert; an uncomfortable encounter with Bruce Weber and his entourage outside of Saint-Eustache; buying it on a shopping spree at a tiny Bretagne boutique with Claude (a desultory affair mercifully terminated when he returned to his ex-wife) etc.

Her nice yoga outfit—a rose patterned Ysé bodysuit with leggings from Falke—wasn't suited to the Bikram she preferred, so she sported Stella Macartney's Adidas collab seamless leggings (moss green) and a matching short sleeve top. She had indoor outfits too, what she called her reading clothes: in the spring/summer she often wore a Yukata kimono she bought in a tiny Tokyo shop her second time there. The Japanese tailor had repaired it twice in the *boro* fashion, one with green and brown calico and once with bright yellow raw silk. Her winter indoor ensemble centered around a grey merino wool Didion dress from Demeulemeester. One of her fondest memories had been reading Jean Rhys in the Didion, an old lambswool throw on her legs, a cup of steaming tea within reach. Her apartment had great winter light. She smiled.

She finished her champagne and took another bite of bread and cheese, dabbing her lip with her napkin. More champagne? How much more time until the flight? The wall clock indicated another hour and a half. She looked around at the family, the JNCO woman and her sleeping dog, and the beautiful black couple in the beautiful clothes. She wanted another glass but didn't want to suffer the ogling of the asshat father with his *sportlich* aggro, so would wait a bit and maybe they'd leave.

Her underwear was functional: sometimes sexy, sometimes less so. While she very much enjoyed the feel of silk on thigh, her smalls never carried the memories of her outer garments. She couldn't, for example, recall what bra and panties the polyester cutout had fallen around. Rui had had a taste for lingerie, which she neither minded nor indulged. She'd worn bras first out of hope and then habit, and now found that La Perla, especially their tulle or lace bralettes, fit her well and so she wore their panties too, replacing as needed at their annual trunk show. She never bothered with even minor repairs and threw them away readily when tattered or soiled. Nightwear was close to underwear and when she slept solo (which was most of the time), she stuck to La Perla or Hesper and Fox pajamas, silk in summer and heavy cotton when colder.

She was careful about shoes, both in the sense of comfort (she walked everywhere and seldom wore anything taller than a kitten heel) and composition (her footwear complemented rather than dominated her look). Like her underwear, memories didn't attach themselves to her shoes, but unlike her underwear, she was polyamorous in her shoe wearing (sneakers from Isabel Marant, ballet flats from Repetto, Oxfords from Weston) and more prudent with their repair. She was mostly indifferent to hats, although she did own a couple of Philip Treacy creations (a white Joan Collins cartwheel from early and a later blue velvet pillbox with tiny animal horns), much preferring a bare head or one of the dozen or so scarves she'd collected from her days at Hermès. She was uninterested in jewelry, and her entire collection was comprised of gifts received (she wasn't sentimental and readily exchanged the ill-chosen) or pieces inherited from her mother and aunt. Her makeup had become more basic over the years, her skin care routine more complex. Her morning makeup usually just meant moisturizer, a little blush, some mascara and lipstick. Evenings, if she were going out, were naturally more elaborate, adding primer, eyeliner and shadow. She'd had been treated to a spa visit to Budapest while doing a show for *Elle* and had gathered skin care products that she could never pronounce but used to this day: cleanser, toner, mask, and skin and eye serum, all supposedly personalized for her smiling face. She'd recently ordered an antioxidant cream from the Hungarian scientists for the new wrinkles that had appeared around her eyebrows, to be mixed according to her file, she supposed.

She didn't put together outfits the day before, as she couldn't be sure what mood she might be in, what image she might desire, or what the light might be the day consequent. In the morning, she'd make her choices based on a combination of composition (color and line), sensory desires (sometimes she wanted the sensation of fine cotton, sometimes wool, sometimes silk) and function (where she was going and what she was going to do). She tried to keep historical recollections out of the equation. For one thing, into each garment was woven a host of different memories, memories that often conflicted and clashed. For example, while the Comme des Garcons cut-out conjured the recollection of exquisite sex with Rui, she'd also worn it for an excruciating cocktail party for an author friend of Robert's, where she'd spilled wine (luckily white) on a pale blue carpet. And she'd worn it out on a late spring evening with Agnes when the weather suddenly turned and she'd nearly frozen. And since she only wore dresses about half the time, more than one article of clothing was usually involved, meaning the possible memories multiplied and could often disagree.

She never shopped vintage and refused to wear used clothing, as she didn't want anyone's past mixed with her own. Even when modeling, she had hesitated wearing pieces other models had worn, even though it was part of the job. She hadn't minded wearing Martin's recycled clothing, like the sweater made of socks (FW 1990) or the images of vintage garments silkscreened on contemporary fabric (SS 1996), as the traces of the historical origin were depersonalized, referring to and honoring fashion's history, not the wearer's. But no, just no, she wouldn't wear used clothes: there was always the possibility that the original wearer was dead.

What was she without clothes? She never thought that her unclothed, naked self was more primary or fundamental. Clothing wasn't something she added to her naked body; it was a primary and constant negotiation between that body (her embodied self) and the world. Clothing (both noun and verb) didn't mask her authentic nature, it gave it form; it didn't protect her being, it *was* her being. It wasn't that she was embarrassed or ashamed by her nude body, but when she did catch glimpses of it (bathing, changing for yoga), it seemed to be wanting (all senses of the word) clothes. If this was shallow or superficial, so be it. No, she refused to think that. Her clothes, her garments, in their history, multiplicity and possibility, were not superficial and the self they helped create thought, felt, and acted as profoundly as any. She was never *au naturale*.

Did she have a life outside of clothes, outside of fashion? What kind of questions was that? Did anyone?

She played with the ratatouille with her fork. Her hunger was largely sated. She would get another glass of champagne before boarding. The ogling father remained across the room, ogling his phone.

Yes, the encounter with Timo and Dunn had disappointed. Timo had been Timo: sympatico, erudite, generous and witty, but she had been surprised at the baffling affinity he appeared to feel for his old friend Jonathan, an affection supposedly initiated by shared history and intellectual milieu, but whose current manifestation seemed stale and one-sided. She had genuinely liked Dunn's book on Castiglione, finding the Comtesse's obsession with dressing, being photographed, and keeping the photographs unseen fascinating and telling. She had hoped that the sensitivity he'd exhibited in that book would be evident in their Margiela encounter, but she found few traces of it in their interactions, and whatever relationship they did have quickly devolved into mutual hostility and mistrust. She found him childishly selfish and unaware, as he undoubtedly found her shopworn and supercilious, indulgence and indulgent, an unnecessary bitch. She had given him a chance, and he had not reciprocated.

Sex seemed to matter less and less to her relationships with men. This didn't make them any more successful.

Speaking of sex with men, she wondered how Carlo was doing. He was younger, indefinitely so, and had a motorcycle. The relationship was in the nascent phase, and she found little so far that offended or irritated. She missed his body, his Basque cooking and his motorcycle, in that order. She hadn't thought of buying him something from New York and wondered if he'd be hurt. If she continued to see him she'd have to obtain some sort of more substantial biker jacket, as the only one she currently owned was the thinnest calfskin number from Bottega Veneta, which wasn't sturdy enough for actual motorcycle rides and was too rarefied even for the temperatures of early fall. She'd need to check her finances when she got home.

The trip had discouraged. She should have known better to trust her past to someone else, someone with no sympathy, someone who didn't listen, someone who ultimately couldn't see. Dunn had no sense of fashion. Not in the way he looked (passive) but in the way he looked (active). Fashion was about creating looks that intrigued, that captured the imagination, that made you wonder about the person whose look you were seeing. What was she like? What was she thinking by wearing that skirt? How did he feel in those shoes? What possessed her to wear both that scarf and that hat? What was it like to be in that body, at that intersection, at that minute of the day? What past experiences did she have to influence those choices? It was all imagination and wonder. Maybe that's what Timo was talking about when he was talking about love. And sometimes, the person you wondered about was you.

And this wonder wasn't immediate, or rather, it wasn't only immediate; it required time. Time to really see, and time that was itself visible. Fashion was time made visible: it was the simultaneous insistence on the now, reference to the past, as well as the intuition of a future. The *marinière* she was wearing *now*, at this very moment, in the slightly muted fluorescent light of the Air France Lounge at JFK, had an undeniable presence. But the history, both personal (Ramona limiting herself to a small glass of wine at Paul Bert) and aesthetic (the transition from French Navy uniform to Parisian fashion mainstay), was just as real. And there was a future implied as well: where would she wear it next? That's what fashion shows, the catwalks, were all about, right? Where could I wear that dress in the future? Maybe that was why fashion models were young: their future was ostentatious, like a Gautier corset or a Schiaparelli broach.

Fashion was time made material. Clotho, Lachesis, Atropos.

The problem was that so few people could see. Dunn couldn't see, that fucker with his family couldn't see, Carlo couldn't see.

Her throat was dry. She looked over at the father sitting with his family. He looked up from his phone, met her gaze and held it. She recognized that look; she had seen it since she was fifteen, from men, mostly men, of anywhere from fourteen to seventy-five. It wasn't a look of lust, necessarily, or even acquisition. It was a look of hunger. She thought back to her Catholic upbringing (she loved visiting *le Sacré Couer*) and the miracle of transubstantiation. That's what he wanted. He wanted her beauty to miraculously save him: he wanted her body to transform his spirit. He wanted her to somehow deliver him from the tedious and pointless sadness of his mundane life. He wasn't looking at her: he couldn't see her. He could only see in her the possibility somehow of being relieved of the drudging monotony of his existence. Jonathan had looked at her and became angry because he knew she couldn't or wouldn't provide the necessary transcendence. Daddy-O over here was looking at her with hunger and hope, what men often defined as visual pleasure.

She dropped her eyes down to her empty glass. Fuck it. She wanted champagne and he wanted a miracle. . .so here's your fucking miracle. She stood abruptly, her napkin falling to the floor. She needed walking music in her head. What was that RuPaul tune she used to walk to, Shady Shady or something like that? Prance girl! Prance I said. Eyes forward. Head aligned with spine. Shoulders up back down and square. Chin up, chin up. Walk a straight line, one foot almost crossing the other. Prance girl. She decided to walk directly toward him and then veer off to the wine cart as she approached his table. One two three four. She didn't want a scene but did want her message understood. She began to walk and exaggerated ever so slightly her hip roll—she was out of practice and was no Yasmeen Ghauri but it was OK. It was like riding a bike. One two three four. Fingers brushing the back of her thighs. Back straight, shoulders square and motionless. No eye contact, no smile. She put her right hand on her hip. One two three four. She looked beyond him; he was definitely looking at her. Looking without seeing. One two three four. Don't be throwing no shade. I just want to get paid. She wasn't going to square up and present. Instead, she veered to her left and walked away, making sure to give him a good view. She didn't break stride, nor did she change the rhythm of her hips. One two three four. Victoria's Secret would never book her for her ass (or for anything really), and the lack of heels didn't help, but he was still looking, she was sure of that; she was sure he was staring at her as she walked away two three four.

Perhaps others were staring as well. Let them. She reached the wine cart and turned; her gaze focused on the champagne bucket. She'd forgotten her glass at her table, but there were plenty more, so she took one from the shelf, filled it from the bottle and relaxed her posture. She could feel his look remain, but it was weak and insubstantial. She looked over at him. He dropped his gaze quickly and turned to one of his children. He was older than she thought at first, mid-forties at least, and his hair was thin and the collar of his track suit was fraying. He looked in need of transcendence. She took a small sip of her wine before walking inconspicuously around the wine cart, away from his table and back to her seat.

She didn't wear clothes as a mirror to reflect back on to whoever was looking. No, she wore clothes to break the mirror, to try to force others to see *her*, to see her not as a miracle or vehicle for their completion, but to see her as a person with her own desires and needs. She dressed to prevent others from projecting clichéd narratives onto her. At least she tried to. As she got older, she was less successful (see Jonathan Dunn).

Maybe, maybe not. She might be overestimating the number of men who still looked at her, Daddy-O notwithstanding. She wasn't invisible, not yet, but she had realized for a while that she was seldom the focal point of any room's attention, perhaps now a stale morsel of bread, a second-rate miracle. That might be a good thing. She didn't know.

She thought of the Belgian clerk at the patisserie and wasn't sure if it proved her point or the opposite.

Clothes changed, people aged, time continued. Stella had told her one late night in London that nothing made her feel alive like walking on the catwalk and being photographed. Stella killed herself five days after she turned fifty. And if fashion was time made material, then time had an ending.

An announcement rang through the lounge: their plane was getting ready to board.

She dressed in order not to die.

The dog got up, shook itself, and yawned.

Perhaps it was as simple as that.

Millie Del'Aria, Paolo Roversi, *Nudi* 1999.

Tsugushara Foujita, "Reclining Nude with Toile de Jouy," 1922, Musée d'Art Moderne de Paris.

Millie Del'Aria, Comme des Garcons, *British Vogue* June 1997, Juergen Teller.

Millie Del'Aria, Comme des Garcons, *I-D* June 1994, Akiri Watanabe.

Millie Del'Aria, Ann Demeulemeester, *Dazed and Confused* No. 3, 1992, Ronald Stoops.

Millie Del'Aria, Martin Margiela, *Paris Vogue* May 2001, Ellen Von Unwerth.

Millie Del'Aria, Hermès, *Vogue Italia* March 1999, Steven Meisel.

CHAPTER FOUR

Winnie Harlow, Iris Van Herpen, Met Gala 2019, anon.

Winnie Harlow, Iris Van Herpen, Met Gala 2099, anon.

Winnie Harlow, Iris Van Herpen, Spring Summer 2000, anon.

Bella Hadid, Various, *Glamour* May 2000, anon.

Anon, "Harajuku Fashion," *Fruits* No 2022, 2019.

Anon, "Japanese Street Fashion," *Vogue Italia* March, 2018, anon.

Anon, "Les Sapeurs of Congo," *Hip Africa* http://hipafrica.com/features/les-sapeurs-of-congo/.

Anon, "Les Sapeurs," *The Chap*, https://thechap.co.uk/2017/12/09/les-sapeurs/.

Leigh Bowery, "1985: Drip-ster," Getty Images.

Leigh Bowery, Still from "The Clothes Show," BBC-1, originally broadcast 17 November, 1986.

CHAPTER FIVE

Marlena Dietrich, "Portrait,' Milton Greene, National Portrait Gallery, 1952.

Lee Miller, "In Hitler's Bathtub," Lee Miller and David E. Scherman, Lee Miller Archives, 1945.

CHAPTER SIX

Edda Ciano, "Portrait," Ghitta Carell, *Archivio Fotografico Fondazione 3M*, circa 1938.

Benito Mussolini, "Portrait," Ghitta Carell, *Archivio Fotografico Fondazione 3M*, 1934.

La Principessa Mafalda di Savoia, "Portrait," Ghitta Carell, *Archivio*

Fotografico Fondazione 3M, 1934.

La Principessa Mafalda di Savoia, "Portrait," Ghitta Carell, *Archivio Fotografico Fondazione 3M*, 1934.

Maria José di Savoia, Principessa di Piemonte, "Portrait," Ghitta Carell, *Archivio Fotografico Fondazione 3M*, 1935.

Tomasso Marinetti, "Portrait," Ghitta Carell, *Archivio Fotografico Fondazione 3M*, 1929.

Contessa Pavoncelli e figli, "Portrait," Ghitta Carell, *Archivio Fotografico Fondazione 3M*, 1935.

Marchesa Patrizi, "Portrait," Ghitta Carell, *Archivio Fotografico Fondazione 3M*, 1940.

Contessa Maria Delfino, "Portrait," Ghitta Carell, *Archivio Fotografico Fondazione 3M*, 1938.

Cardinal Francis Joseph Spellman, "Portrait," Ghitta Carell, *Archivio Fotografico Fondazione 3M*, 1940.

Walt Disney, "Portrait," Ghitta Carell, *Archivio Fotografico Fondazione 3M*, 1935.

Benito Mussolini, "Portrait," Ghitta Carell, *Archivio Fotografico Fondazione 3M*, 1933.

Benito Mussolini, "Portrait," Ghitta Carell, *Archivio Fotografico Fondazione 3M*, 1938.

Contessa Arrivabene, "Portrait," Ghitta Carell, *Archivio Fotografico Fondazione 3M*, 1934.

Adolf Hitler, "Portrait," Henrich Hoffman Studio, US National Archives 1932.

Adolf Hitler and Hermann Goering, "Return to Berlin," anon., Getty Images, 1940.

Adolf Hitler, "Adolf Hitler addresses a rally of the SA," Heinrich Hoffmann Studio, US Holocaust Museum, 1933.

Anon, "*Wehrmacht* soldiers shooting Polish civilians in a reprisal," anon, 1939.

Anon, "Camp Guards greet train at Treblinka," anon. US National Archives 1943.

Luchino Visconti, "Portrait," Ghitta Carell, *Archivio Fotografico Fondazione 3M*, 1933.

Chapter Seven
Millie Del'Aria, Martin Margiela, Spring Summer 1990, Jean-Claude Cautausse.

Millie Del'Aria, Martin Margiela, Fall Winter 1995, Anders Edström.
Stella Tennant and Millie Del'Aria, untitled, Mark Borthwick, private collection, circa 1999.
Deirdre Jensen and Millie Del'Aria, Dolce and Gabana, *Vanity Fair* August 2001, Ellen von Unwerth.
Millie Del'Aria, Hermès, Fall Winter 2002, anon.
Millie Del'Aria, Hermès, *Vogue Paris* September 1999, Jordan Brown.
Millie Del'Aria, Comme des Garcons, Spring Summer 2003, Paolo Roversi.

CHAPTER EIGHT
Charlize Theron, Cover, *Vogue* April 2022.

Acknowledgements

This book would not exist if not for the generosity of a number of colleagues, experts and friends. I would like to thank the following: Emily Ripley for the wonderful conversations and introduction to the culture; Alexandre Samson for his kindness and brilliance; Megan O'Connell for decades of inspiring friendship and helping me find Proust's grave; Elissa Author for her luminous eye and spirit; Karan Rinaldo, Collections Manager Photographs and Marci Morimoto, Associate Collections Manager at The Costume Institute of The Metropolitan Museum of Art for their guidance and patience; Bliss Foster for a really fucking smart series on Margiela's work; Ryan Chang for long distance convos and a fine sense of style; the two Isabels, Geary-Phelps and Beeman, for my favorite liquor off the top shelf; Monica Jae Yeon Moon at *Vestoj* for being a perfect editor; Jeff Cox for believing in this project; Katherine Woods and Loie Rawding for making me proud as hell; Holly Woodsome Sroymalai for years of giggles and assistance; Caroline Evans and Gwenda-Linn Grewal for writing absolutely brilliant books; Curtis White for the perfectly timed; Tod Thilleman for indefatigable vision; Patrick Greaney for his intellectual influence; Marco Breuer for presence and mind; and Elisabeth Sheffield for everything.

Thanks to the University of Colorado English Department, the University of Colorado Arts and Science's Fund for Excellence and Committee on Arts and Humanities for providing the funding for archival research.

Chapter Four is indebted to the following texts (at least):

Fredrich Nietzsche, "On Truth and Lie in the Extramoral Sense," *The Will to Power* and *Genealogy of Morals*.
Valerie Steele, "The F-word," *Lingua franca* (April 1991): 17-20.
Gwenda-Linn Grewal, *Fashion | Sense: On Philosophy and Fashion.*

An edited excerpt from Chapter 4 recently appeared at *Vestoj*:

http://vestoj.com/fashionietzsche/

Cover Photo:
Five Girls in a Room in Pigalle, Paris—
© Deborah Turbeville/MUUS Collection